OBSESSION

Memories of Sorrow Book 1

Ang Roffe

Studio Fantasy Publishing

CONTENTS

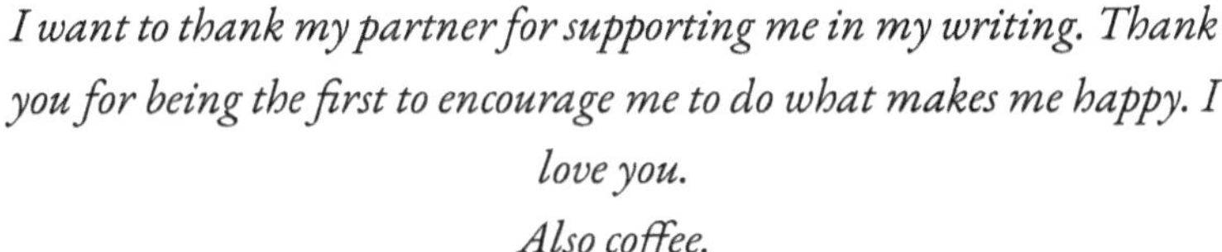

I want to thank my partner for supporting me in my writing. Thank you for being the first to encourage me to do what makes me happy. I love you.
Also coffee.

Preface

I've always had dozens of storylines running through my head. When I first started to write, I thought this would give me an opportunity to share scary and weird stories that I had in my mind.

In reality, this book turned out to be so much more.

Through the weaving of fantasy and horror ideas, this book helped me explore my own traumatic background. Because of this, Obsession includes topics such as the following:

- Familial Violence

- Emotional and Psychological Trauma

- Graphic Violence and Death

Chapter 1

His blank eyes stare back into mine. Streams of blood stain the sides of his face from where his eyeballs had been dragged out of their sockets. One of them lies on the grass next to his body.

"What the fuck is this?"

Arvir's deep voice breaks my attention away from the drawing he's holding in his hand.

"It's nothing, it's just a drawing."

"You call this just a drawing? Why do I look like this? Are you threatening me?"

"No! Of course not, it's just a drawing. A doodle I made in class. Don't you sometimes get distracted during class?"

His fist slams against the glass behind me. The force from his hand causes the glass to shake.

His body towers over mine. One lone bead of sweat dangles from his forehead. His face is red and flustered.

He's going to do something. I know it.

With one hand behind my back, I conjure a small dart and tighten my grip around it.

His hand rises to my neck. I swing my arm forward, pretending to be surprised.

The tiny dart digs itself into his biceps, only noticeable by its glistening in the sunlight. It digs itself deeper until it disappears.

He slams my back against the window.

"You have one last chance to tell me. What is this?"

I should calm him down. I can probably find something to say to get him to back off. Some way to get out of this situation. But I want to see what happens.

And I kind of want to see him get hurt.

I curl my lips into a grin. "I saw how you're going to die. And I drew it. That's your future."

His fist connects with my nose, sending my head flying back against the glass. I can hear the cracking sound of my nose breaking.

"Arvir!" Dean Nula's voice rings in my ears before I can get to my feet. "What's going on here? What did you do to him?"

Ms. Nula's frame fills the doorway, and her flats click against the floor as she pushes past the scattered desks. Her black hair combed to the side bounces up and down as she approaches us.

What a disappointment. If only she could have given us a few more minutes.

He backs away from me, holding his hands up in front of him. "This isn't my fault. He's the one who started it, Ms. Nula. I swear, look at what I found."

"I don't care what you found, Arvir. Oyster Harbor Academy has a zero tolerance policy for violence. It's within my authority to expel you from this university."

Her eyes focus on the paper he's waving in front of her. She grabs it. As she inspects it, her face twists and she glances at me.

"You. To my office now." She says to Arvir, still holding the drawing in her hand.

He looks like he's about to protest, but reaches to grab his backpack from the floor before leaving the classroom.

She pulls out the radio from her back pocket.

"Mr. Ikontye, please call Ms. Vilon Jahlo to the office to meet with her son. Please also alert Ms. Hin Kuen to come as soon as she can make it. Her son was also involved in the incident."

"Yes, ma'am."

I pull myself to my feet, holding my sleeve to my nose to stop the bleeding.

"Shion, can you please explain what this is to me?"

"It's nothing. I told Arvir this. It's just a drawing."

She motions for me to sit, and she pulls up a chair next to mine. The chair creaks under the weight of her muscular frame, and she struggles to fit herself in between the desk and seat.

"Why do you have a drawing like this? Don't you think that the other students are going to be afraid if they see you with this?"

"I don't really care what the other students think."

She sighs, and her head falls into her hands. "Look, Shion. For the past few years I've known you, you've always been an amazing student. All of your professors would agree with me on that. But this year, something is different about you. Some of the other students, they don't feel comfortable around you. You scare a lot of them. And not only the students, either."

I grip the side of my desk.

"Please, just go clean yourself up and meet us in the office. We will discuss what will happen later."

She stands from her chair, pausing for a moment before reaching down to grab my shoulder.

"I'm worried about you. You've changed. And not in a good way."

...

I splash the cold water onto my face. After a few rough rubs on the bloodstains, they finally wash away into the sink.

When I turn the knob of the paper towel dispenser, nothing comes out.

What a surprise. I don't even remember the last time they were filled.

The rest of the restroom is a mess, and it looks like Mr. Ikontye hasn't cleaned it in weeks. Graffiti covers every stall door. The stall door at the end is still broken from its hinge, causing it to twist inward.

Water stains the floor surrounding the sinks. The thick layer of dust on the mirror clouds my reflection.

I scrunch my nose. As I move it, the putrid odor of feces fills my nostrils. One of the toilets must be clogged again.

Looking back, I realize taunting Arvir was a mistake. I hope no one questions how my nose healed so quickly.

Satisfied with my appearance, I leave the restroom and head down to the main office.

When I enter the waiting room, Mr. Ikontye is just hanging up the phone.

Did Mom answer? Or was she too busy to pick up?

His long brown hair is tied back in a tangled mess. Thin streaks of hair plaster against his face. Dark bags line his eyes, and it looks like he hasn't slept in days.

"Hello Shion! What brings you in here today? I heard you got in an altercation with another student? Everything all right?"

"Yeah, nothing I can't deal with. I'll let you know how it goes."

The dean notices me through the small window on her office door and she reaches down to press the button to let me in. When I step inside, Arvir is sitting in one chair. In the other, I recognize Ms. Jahlo as another teacher from the school.

She always looked young, not someone that would already have a child that's a full-grown adult. She tightens her grip on the chair arm, tapping her perfectly manicured fingernails. Her matching red dress is tight against her body. The only signs of her age are the growing lines of gray in her curled hair.

I never had her as a professor before, but both Ariy and Fasmoh have her this year. Fasmoh always mentioned that she seemed to give Arvir special attention.

Ms. Jahlo holds out my drawing to me. "Arvir tells me this fell from your backpack. Can you explain this to me, please?"

"It's just a drawing. You know, sometimes I get bored in class and need something to keep myself busy."

Arvir leans over his mom's chair. "No, he's lying! Why don't you tell them what you said to me earlier?" His mom raises a frail hand to his arm and whispers something into his ear. He falls back into his seat.

The three of them look at me, waiting for a response.

"I didn't mean what I said. It was a joke. I can't actually see the future. If I could, I wouldn't be stuck in this shithole, anyway." My last comment comes out much louder than I planned, and Ms. Nula shoots me a glare.

"This place you call a shithole is one of the few places that can give you a future. But if that's how you feel, then I can just expel you from the school and you won't have to be stuck here anymore. Is that what you want?"

I shake my head. "No, sorry. It's just a drawing. There's no deeper meaning behind it, I promise."

"I trust you." When Ms. Jahlo says this, Arvir's mouth falls open, and he glares at her. Ms. Nula has a similar look on her face. The look disappears from her face, and she replaces it with a small smile.

"I noticed that they both have the same first morning class, so I will move Arvir from the class immediately."

"Actually, why don't you move them both into my class in the morning? That way, I can keep an eye on both of them to make sure that there are no more issues between them." Ms. Nula's suggestion makes my stomach twist into a knot.

"Of course. Why don't we get that taken care of now? Shion, you are free to leave for your next class. If your professor asks, let them know you were in my office."

By the time I leave the office, Mr. Ikontye is already gone. Probably to deal with another incident in the school.

As I'm about to open the front doors of the school, a loud crack echoes. I turn back to look into Ms. Nula's office.

I forgot about Arvir.

His head falls forward, hand under his nose. When he pulls his hand away, blood is gushing from his nose.

Before I walk out, Ms. Nula's wide eyes meet mine.

CHAPTER 2

"Where are you going?"

I turn back towards the staircase leading up to the school. Ariy is standing in the open doorway.

She walks down the front steps, taking two at a time to catch up to me. With each step she takes, her glasses bounce up and down on the bridge of her nose, and she raises a hand to steady them. A few strands of her dyed red bangs hang over her face.

"I'm going home."

"Right now? Don't you still have another class?"

I shrug. "What's the point?"

"The end of the year review is coming. If they find out that you've been skipping classes, then they're going to give you a negative review. That's going to hurt your chances with the scholarship awards next week."

"Well, I guess that makes it easier for you to win, right?"

She snorts out a laugh. "The only ones you qualify for aren't even close to my league. I'm in the running for the Honor of the Guard scholarship. And I'm going to win." The smirk on her face softens. "Won't your mom get mad at you?"

"What do I care? We're adults. She will not control my life anymore."

The bell rings, catching Ariy off guard. Her face of panic quickly disappears.

"Isn't being late going to hurt your chances?" I say with exaggerated sarcasm.

"The school doesn't really care what I do anymore, especially once I win." She pauses for a moment, clearing her throat. "But I've been worried about you. Fasmoh and I, we've both been worried about you. We feel like we barely see you much anymore."

"I'm sorry. I've been busy."

"You're always busy."

I turn away towards the street. Even though it's barely in the afternoon, the thick fog over the area blocks out much of the sun. None of the streetlights are on. I can't tell if it's because it's still too early or if they're all broken.

She takes a step forward, closing the gap between us. Her voice falls to a whisper. "You should really come join us after school one of these days. I know you said you don't believe in magic, but we might find something that can help you. Even with your personal issues."

"Magic?" I realize that my voice is loud, but luckily no one is around to hear us.

Her face scrunches up, and she looks hurt. "We kept asking you if you wanted to try some spells out with us last year, remember? You always said you were too busy or that your mom wouldn't let you go."

That's right. I forgot they always practiced magic together after school. Or at least they tried to. But this time, her offer intrigues me. "You know what? Sure, let's do it."

"Really? Okay, great! I'll check in with Fasmoh later. We can go to my place. My parents won't be home for another few weeks, anyway."

She turns back to the school, running up the steps. She waves at me as the large doors slam behind her.

...

As I walk up the driveway to my house, bright lights flash behind me.

My heart sinks into my chest. She's home already? She must have left work right when she got to Mr. Ikontye's car.

Mom parks her car slanted in the driveway before stepping from the car. As she slams the front door, her long, black hair nearly gets caught.

"Shion? What's going on? Your school called me earlier and left a voicemail. They said there was an incident involving you and another student?"

"It's nothing, Mom, just stuff going on at school. Don't worry about it."

"I am worried about it. I'm your mother. You need to tell me everything that is going on in your life."

I turn, pushing my way through the front door. She quickly chases after me, gripping my wrist. Her dark brown eyes glare up into mine. Underneath her straight cut bangs, I can see her furrowed eyebrows.

"Where are you going? I'm not done talking to you."

"Well, I'm done talking to you. This is none of your business. I've been an adult for several years already and you still treat me like a kid. Will you leave me alone for once?"

"No matter how old you are, you're still my son and I need to know what is going on in your life. If something happens, I need to know exactly what happens. You are my business."

I can hear how labored her breathing is. She's not used to me talking back to her this much. Not yet.

"Arvir saw a drawing I had and got offended. Not my fault. It was just a drawing. He's the one who punched me, anyway. Why am I the one getting into trouble?"

"Oh, honey." She grabs me in a tight hug, and I struggle to free myself from her arms. "Are you okay? Where did he punch you? Does it hurt?"

"I told you, I'm fine."

She sighs before pushing me away.

"You should talk to him. Clear things up. Him and his mom are good people, and I want you to have a good relationship with them. Maybe even a friendship?"

The involuntary groan I let out is much louder than I expect. "He's not my friend, and he never will be. Can you stop bringing this up? I don't need you to tell me to be more social or make more friends. This is my life."

"Shion, I'm just worried about you. You've been spending so much time in your room all alone, doing nothing with your life. I want to make sure that you're having social interactions with others. It never hurts to network, especially since you're going to work soon."

"How would you even know what I do? You're never home! All you do is work all day and all night. And you have the audacity to tell me that my life is a waste?"

The hurt spreads across her face, and my muscles tense up. In the silence between us, I take it as an opportunity to flee to my bedroom.

I drop my stuff onto the floor and fall face forward onto my bed. The cold soft blanket covers my body and all I want to do is close my eyes and never wake.

But I have work to do.

It takes several minutes for me to force myself from the comfort of my bed. I walk over to open my closet, pulling out scattered objects and setting them on the floor outside of the closet.

Once there's enough space, I step inside. It's dark, but small. I place my hand against the wooden wall at the opposite end, still partially damp from the last time I was here.

Pulling out the small pocket knife from my keys, I dig the blade into my palm, feeling the warm blood spread on my hand.

CHAPTER 3

My hand leaves another bloody handprint on the wall, nearly covering the previous mark.

The outline of my hand spreads outward. As it spreads, small wisps of gray light flick towards my body. As the blood grows in size, so does the light.

With each step forward I take, the whips of light reach forward. Everywhere they touch, they leave a cold imprint. Soon, they engulf my entire body. All around me is gray and cold.

Light breaks through the darkness, ray by ray. As the darkness slowly dissipates, the temperature rises to normal.

I'm back in my hideout.

The interior looks like a cavern. Pillars surround the room, holding the rocky ceiling above. Uneven cobblestone steps lead down to the center, where a small room surrounded by stone arches waits for me.

When I enter the room, the opposite end is closed off. A long table lines the wall, with various tools and bottles. To either sides of me are tall shelves holding labeled jars and bowls. Most of them are ingredients I came across in the forest, but a few of them were more difficult to get.

I step over to a shelf, grabbing my journal from where I left it. I flip through a few pages until I find the one I'm looking for. Once I find it, I set the book down on the table to read the instructions. Most of the ingredients I need are already nearby, but some I have to dig through on the shelves.

Underneath the table is a small wooden chest. I pick it up and set it on the table, and immediately the scent of rotten flesh hits me. I push it to the side while I prepare the ingredients.

Jar after jar, I pour the ingredients into a bowl. Wooden spoon in hand, I mash them together until they mix into a fine powder. I pour some of the black liquid that I had to steal from the hospital a few weeks ago. As each drop hits the powder, large black bubbles start to form and grow.

I step back to avoid the splash each time they pop. When it finally settles, I squeeze a few drops of blood into it.

I quickly flip open the chest and cough a few times to clear my throat. The otter's body has decayed. When I pick it up by the leg, a few maggots fall from the tire tracks on its hind leg.

I stick my finger into the liquid and draw a circle around the otter's body. With the picture of the scroll in my mind, I copy the intricate strokes and patterns of the symbol around.

The rancid odor fills my nose as I work.

A faint pounding comes from behind me. The sound is coming from the stone entrance, and it echoes through the cave.

Mom must be knocking at my door.

I quickly set everything down, tightening the lids on all the ingredients. Taking two steps at a time, I reach the top of the staircase and throw myself into the stone wall. My shoulder hits the soft floor of my closet, and I turn to watch as the circle of blood behind me shrinks slowly.

But when I open my bedroom door, it's not her.

Dad? What's he doing here?

He looks like he's wearing the same jeans and long sleeve t-shirt that he was wearing the last time I saw him. I don't even remember when that was, but I recognize the same hole underneath his collar.

Caked dirt lines at the bottom of his shoes. I wonder if Mom's going to notice all the dirt he tracked in.

"You got in trouble at school today. Again."

It's not a question. I already heard enough lectures today, and I definitely don't care what he has to say.

But how did he find out about it? It's not like Mom would have told him.

"Don't worry about it. Nothing happened."

An awkward silence passes between us, and he shifts his weight from foot to foot. "Look, I don't know what's going on with you, nor do I really care. But you better not do anything that causes any problems for me, understand that? If I have to hear that you're getting in any more trouble, then we've got a problem."

"How do you plan to find out about that if you're never here?"

His head falls forward a little, and he shakes his head. "I don't need this attitude from you. I have more important things to deal with. All I'm saying is I better not hear about this again. I've got work to do."

He turns to walk away. His walk is slow, and his body leans heavily to each side. Each step seems to tire him.

"Not staying for dinner, then?" But he ignores me and turns down the stairs.

I don't know why he seems so tired all the time or where he is every day. It's not like he has a job.

No matter how much he tries to be a parent, he never will be.

Besides the clicking of the lock on my door, there's a tiny yelp. Did that come from the closet?

I stand in front of the sliding door, waiting to see if another noise comes. Soon, a clawing sound comes from the bottom of the wood.

It's already finished? And how did it get out? Did I leave the portal open by accident?

When I pull it open, the otter bolts out of my closet, jumping onto my bed. He's running around in circles, and I notice that its skin is hanging from one of its legs..

As the resurrected otter shivers against the bed frame, his tiny bones rattle.

"Come here, buddy." I gently grab his loose skin, shaking it free from his leg. It slides off with little resistance.

When he's finally free, he runs around the room a few times in circles before rubbing up against my leg. The jagged edges of his broken hind leg scratch against my leg.

He jumps up at me from the ground, yelping each time. On the third jump, I grab him and hold him up against my shoulder.

"I'm going to call you Luna."

Chapter 4

With my head tilted up towards the sky, I close my eyes and inhale a deep breath. The fresh, woody scent fills my lungs. My chest burns until I release the air from my lungs.

The air has an earthy taste to it. It has a hint of sweetness to it. Blueberries. Near the ground, mushrooms grow on fallen logs and I can make out different small fruit plants.

It's nice being back.

Though this trail takes longer than the neighborhood streets to get to the academy, it always used to be a relaxing calm before the chaos of school.

I lift my head to the treetops as I walk. The bright rays of morning light shine through the branches, washing over me.

My shoes squish in the shallow mud. I'll have to remember to clean them before I get home.

I squint my eyes at the high tree branches in the tree. There's something hanging from it.

A small puddle on the ground causes me to stop. It looks like blood. I kneel forward, about to test the liquid, when another drop falls from the tree. It's thick and red.

Arvir's blood?

It has to be. Even though I can't see that high up, the blood must be dripping from one of his body parts.

But why is this happening? It's too soon.

I step around the tree, making sure not to leave a footprint. I can see it in the clearing behind the tree.

It's Arvir's torso. But only his torso. I step around it to get a look at the front of his body.

His face is exactly how it was in my drawing. His eyeless eyes look back into mine, and one of his eyeballs lies on the floor, the brown eye pointed towards one of the surrounding trees.

Something hits my shoulder. It feels moist, like a raindrop.

When I look up, I see them. Several ropes hang from the treetops. Some are high, some are closer to the ground. From one hangs an arm. On another one, there's a leg.

Both Arvir's.

I kneel to the ground, unzipping my backpack. Using one of the plastic boxes and a leaf, I scoop up the eyeball and seal the box before replacing it.

I need to get this home as soon as possible.

But I'm close to the school. And school starts soon. If I'm late and they find the body today, that might make me look even more suspicious.

Especially now that Ms. Nula has my drawing.

I need to be there on time and pretend that everything is fine.

A few minutes later, I reach the door to the school. I make my way up to my new first class, and I see Ms. Jahlo is sitting at her desk.

She turns to me right as I enter the room. She must have been waiting for me.

"What happened to my son yesterday?"

I struggle to keep my breath steady. What is she talking about? Did she already know he was dead? Did someone find his body?

Why is she still at work?

"Uhm... something happened yesterday? What are you talking about? I haven't seen him since I left the school."

"That is what I mean. After you left, something happened. Somehow, his nose broke."

"Oh, no. Is he okay? Did he fall?" I respond, trying to sound concerned.

"He didn't fall. Ms. Nula told me what she saw after we took him home last night. She told me you were watching through the window when it happened. How can you explain something like that?"

"I have no idea what you're talking about. Maybe he accidentally hit himself or something." We stare at each other for a few moments before I turn away. I realize I went a little overboard during our fight, but it was Arvir's fault.

And now he's dead.

"I know what you are." Her voice is low, but loud enough for me to hear.

I walk to the back of the classroom. At least Fasmoh's here.

"What was that about?" She asks as I take the seat behind her, not looking away from her phone.

"Oh, it was nothing. She was just asking me something." When I look at her, I notice what she's wearing. Rather than the typical dark blue one she wore, this one was a bright pink with small gems creating patterns on the back. "New khimar? It looks nice."

She scoffs.

"You doing all right?"

"I've worn this for the past week."

My face twists into a look of shame and guilt. "Oh, sorry. We haven't seen each other much."

"Yep."

Today she seems quiet.

I know I've been neglecting my friends for the past few weeks, but I don't have time for them. It is nice to be together again, but I'm here for one reason. I can't waste my time with friendships.

I still feel bad though.

"So, yesterday Ariy invited me to join you two with your magic night one of these days. Maybe we can catch up then?"

"She told me."

"Great."

I want to press the conversation further. But I look at my backpack.

There's a few more hours to lunch, and I can sneak away then. I can't keep this on me.

Especially if they discover Arvir's body.

Once the bell rings, Ms. Jahlo is standing in the front, glancing over the class. I avoid her eyes as she looks in my direction, and turn back right as she's looking at another student.

"Relli? Have you seen Arvir this morning?"

The student next to me turns. Their long blonde hair brushes against my backpack, and I slide it underneath my desk with my foot. "No, Ma'am, not at all this morning. Doesn't he come with you in the mornings?"

She shakes her head. "I had to be here early today, and he wanted to sleep in. Maybe he's just running a little late."

The phone on her desk rings, and she hurries over to pick it up. She holds the phone close to her ear and motions for silence.

"Now? But what about class?" She nods before setting the phone on the receiver.

"Students, please get started on the assignment posted online. The office called me down to discuss something, but I'll be right back."

Once she leaves, none of the students pull out their laptops to work on the assignment. None of them besides Ariy.

Fasmoh rises from her desk, sliding into the empty seat next to Ariy. "What are you doing?" When Ariy turns, her dark red ponytail almost hits Fasmoh in the face.

"We have an assignment to do, and I need to get a good grade in this class. Did you hear about the scholarship ceremony? The head of the Royal Guardians needs more candidates, so they're raising the amount of each award. The Honor of the Guard award is now $300,000!"

"Oh, wow. That's a lot." I say, trying to insert myself into the conversation. Fasmoh turns away from me, looking back at Ariy.

"Yes, yes, I know. That's why I'm so excited that you're going to join us tomorrow. We're going to find a spell to help me win it. And of course, find spells for whatever the two of you want, obviously. Unless it's about the scholarship. Because that's already taken."

I grin. "Don't worry, I have no plans to take that scholarship from you."

"So you're actually joining us? You're not too busy tomorrow?" Fasmoh's voice has a hint of accusation in it.

"Yeah, why not? It sounds fun." Ms. Jahlo still hasn't come back. I wonder what the urgent incident was that she had to deal with.

Did they find him?

The door opens, and silence falls through the class. Several students move back to their own seats. A few of them pretend to type away at their computers.

Instead of our teacher, though, it's Ms. Nula who walks through the door.

"Shion, please come with me."

Ariy and Fasmoh look at me before I follow her out of the room.

She takes me down to her office, and I notice a tall man sitting in front of her desk. The red symbol of the Royal Guardians of Coniston is embroidered on the right chest of his uniform.

"Mr. Kuen, please take a seat. This is Royal Guardian Vahreld. He requested to speak to you."

The man moves the paper from his lap, standing to shake my hand. I take it, and his hand grips mine.

"Hey, it's Shion, right?" He smiles before letting go.

When I take the seat next to him, he leans back and runs his hand through his shaved head.

"I was wondering if you have time to talk with me? I know you're supposed to be in class right now, but there's an incident I wanted to clear up."

"Of course."

He's holding a photocopy of my drawing in front of him. "Could you explain this to me?"

"Well, as I had told the dean already, the drawing was just that. A drawing. It means nothing."

Before he can respond, Ms. Nula speaks up. "That's not what you said to Arvir yesterday. You told him you saw how he was going to die. And the day after, someone finds his body in the woods? How did you know this was going to happen?" Her eyes squint accusingly at me. "Either you have magic, or you're the one who killed him."

"Dean," Vahreld says, "could you leave us for a few minutes? I need to discuss this with Shion alone."

She opens her mouth in protest, but decides against it. As she walks out, I can feel her glare on the back of my head.

"Well, it looks like I can't hide it anymore. Your classmate was found dead." He turns the drawing back to face him, examining it. "What inspired you to draw something like this?"

"Nothing. I don't know, I kind of just imagined it and drew it."

He leans forward and reaches into his pocket to pull out his phone. He taps away at the screen before turning it towards me.

It's a picture of Arvir. In the woods. How the picture was taken almost matches my drawing. Except for his missing eye.

"So you don't have an explanation of why your drawing looks like the crime scene?"

My mouth falls open in feigned surprise. "I promise you, I have no idea what happened to him. It's just a coincidence."

He leans forward, mouth inches from my ear. "I trust you. I know you didn't do this. But I also know you're hiding something from me." He leans forward, whispering into my ear. "She was right, wasn't she? About the magic?"

"I don't know what you're talking about."

"All you need to know for now is that I know more about you than you think. I know you're stronger than you let others know. I know you can do things that others can't."

He crosses his arms before leaning back into his chair to continue. "You ever think about joining the academy? You could leave the school right now and never have to come back. We can take care of you and your mom, so you'd never have to worry about money again."

He pulls a card from his pocket, handing it over to me. It has information about the Honor of the Guard scholarship, including a website for the application and the requirements. Reading through them, I don't meet a lot of them.

"Look into this. It would be a valuable opportunity for you and your mom. We could use someone like you. Someone with real power."

His offer catches me off guard.

"Wait, if you think I'm hiding some kind of magic, why would you want me to be a part of the guard? I thought the Royal Guardians look down on magic?"

"Let's just say there are some of us that don't fully agree with all the ideals of the Royal Guardians. While some think we need to eradicate all forms of magic from Coniston, there are a few of us who realize that will be an impossible task." A grin crosses his face. "How can we expect to control those with magic if we don't have magic?"

He walks over to the door, resting his hand against the door handle. "Think about what I said. I might be the only one who can protect you. I'll keep the details of Arvir's death hidden, so that no one will tie your drawing to his death. But I don't know how long I'll be able to keep it up. Be careful."

After he leaves, I drop the card into the trash can.

CHAPTER 5

My right arm starts to buckle underneath the weight of the candle.

How much longer do they want me to hold this for?

The three of us are standing in a circle, holding long black candles in each hand. Part of my candle melts, burning my hand. The wax hardens, relieving the stinging pain.

Ariy and Fasmoh are chanting some words from pieces of paper that Ariy printed from the internet.

I bite my lower lip, trying to stop myself from laughing. Luckily, the other two don't notice. Once the other two lower their candles, we blow them out before setting them on the table.

"So, how often do the two of you do this?"

"We have to do this at least once a week. Otherwise, the spells lose their potency. We have to keep recasting them if we want them to work." Ariy's voice is excited. Behind her, Fasmoh turns her head to the side.

"And have they worked for you in the past?" I direct my question towards Fasmoh, but Ariy is the one who answers.

"Of course they have. Ever wonder why no one seems to bother us? About anything? It's also been helping me get much better marks in my classes. I'm definitely going to win the Honor of the Guard."

"Ahh, of course." Fasmoh hears my sarcasm and glares at me.

I hate how mad she is at me.

"How do you feel after that?" Ariy leans in.

"The same, I guess."

"You won't really feel much of it at first. Sometimes you feel nothing."

"Then how do you know it works?"

Ariy smiles.

"It works. You'll see."

"What about Shion? We should do a spell for you, too. That was the point of inviting him here, right?" Fasmoh finally speaks up. It's the first time she's addressed me since we've started.

I want to say yes, to clear things up between Fasmoh and me. I hope that spending more time with them doing what they enjoy will bring us back together.

But I don't have the time right now. And it won't make a difference.

"Thanks, but how about next time? I really need to get home before my parents worry about me. But I appreciate it."

"Of course, if you ever want to learn more or you want a refresh on the spell you're always welcome back."

We make our way to the front door, and I step out. To my surprise, Fasmoh follows me.

"I think I'm going home, too. It's getting dark out, and if there is a murderer, it might be best if the two of us walk home together.

After we say our goodbyes, Fasmoh and I walk down the sidewalk. A chilly breeze passes, causing goosebumps on my shoulders. One of the lone working street lights above us flickers.

"So, cool magic, huh?"

She snorts. "You don't actually believe in that stuff, do you?"

"Yeah, I do. Well, maybe not reading off spells from a website type of magic, but I think magic is real. Ariy seems to believe in it, too. I thought you did."

She rolls her eyes. "I don't know. I mean, it's fun and all, but it's not real. Coincidences happen all the time. Ariy casts a spell that helps her do well on a hard test, and the next day she gets a good grade on it."

"But they don't work for you?"

"Nope."

She pauses, looking up at the sky.

"I do sometimes wish it were real, you know what I mean? I just think magic could just fix so many problems for me. For my family. I'm not saying Arvir's death isn't sad, but so many people in our town have been dying. So many people in the world."

When she turns back, her eyes glisten from the tears building up.

"Imagine what we could do if it were real."

"Well, we'll see if it works when the serial killer gets us, huh?"

She laughs, punching my shoulder. I smile back at her, hiding the pain from my face.

This feels normal.

"Something will work for you. I guarantee it. You just gotta believe in yourself."

"Oh yeah, totally. I'll tell you if something magical happens to me." She emphasizes the word magical by holding her hands up and twirling her fingers.

I laugh. We continue down the sidewalk, and I stop in front of her house. It towers over the ones next to it, and the fresh coat of blue paint stands out in comparison to the faded colors of the other houses.

"Let's go to your place. I'll drop you off and come back."

"Are you sure? You want to walk alone?" Her lack of reaction tells me to keep moving. "Thanks."

We walk another block in an awkward silence. I want to say something, but I can't seem to find the right words.

"Hey Fasmoh? Look, I'm sorry. That stuff you said earlier? You're right. I have been neglectful of our friendship. I've just been dealing with a lot of stuff right now, you know? But I promise, I'll be a better friend. To both of you."

"We've all been going through stuff. Not just you."

"Of course I know that everyone is going through some stuff. I'm just saying that I'm sorry if sometimes I don't notice what's going on with you two. Sometimes it's hard to be there for you."

"You weren't there for me when she died." Her body falls against me into my arms, and she tightens her grip against my back. "I called you... From the hospital. No one else could make it to be there with me. Not dad, not my brother. I needed you."

"I'm so sorry, Fasmoh. I'm so sorry. From now on, I will be here for you. Always."

I grip her tighter.

...

When we finally reach my house, we say our goodbyes. I wave at her from the doorway. Once I'm inside, I watch her turn the corner through the eyehole.

How did her mom die already? Everything just seems... wrong. Both she and Arvir were killed much earlier than they should have been. What's going on here?

I need to figure out what's going on. Now. Before it's too late.

By the time I get to my closet door, Luna is already clawing at the door. When I open it, he jumps out at me. His bones dig into my leg as he climbs up my body.

"Hey buddy. Sorry I took so long to come back today. I'll try to be back sooner next time."

As I slip into the closet, I look back at him. He looks back up at me expectantly, and his tail bone slaps against the wall.

"You should probably stay here for now. You don't want to be in there.

I descend the staircase in my hideout down to the center floor, grabbing a jar from the table. The formaldehyde has a strong, pungent odor that I can smell through the lid.

It's only been a day since I put Arvir's eye into the solution, but it's already expanded to nearly twice its size. The whites of his eye have turned a cloudy gray.

It's almost ready.

Chapter 6

My anxiety has never been this high in my life.

A few of the nights I don't even remember falling asleep. Only tossing and turning to find a comfortable position to sleep in.

School hasn't been any better.

Rumors spread through the school about Arvir's death. By now, everyone already heard about me and my drawing. Staff and students either ignore me or actively try to avoid me when they see me coming down the hallway.

Ms. Jahlo is still gone. No one mentioned where she's been, but we all know. How could she come back to school after such a gruesome thing happened to her son?

I am glad about her absence. How would she react to me still at the academy? If everyone else wants me expelled, what does she want to happen to me?

I roll out of bed and throw on a pair of sweatpants and a long sleeve shirt. My feet drag against the carpet as I slowly make my way down the stairs.

"Good morning, honey!"

Her voice catches me off guard, and I swing around. She's standing in the middle of the kitchen, still dressed in her long bathrobe.

Dark black liquid drips from the coffee maker, and I can smell the bitterness from here.

"Mom? What are you doing here? Shouldn't you be at work right now?"

"I requested a few days off of work and my boss finally accepted it. I'm going to be able to stay home and give you the attention that you need."

"You didn't have to."

"I don't have to, but I want to. I want to make sure that everything is okay with you. Especially with what happened to your classmate. I'll be here to protect you." She grabs a second cup of coffee, filling both of them before handing me one.

Trying to figure out who the killer is will be much more difficult with her around.

We sit at the dining table sipping at the coffee while watching the news on the small TV in the corner of the room.

I've been keeping up to date on the news around our town just in case any more murders happened, but the past few days have been pretty quiet. Watching the news today is so much different from my mom watching me the whole time. Every time I try to focus on what the reporter is saying, I can feel her eyes on the side of my head.

My drawing pops up in the center of the screen.

Fuck.

"Our sources have informed us that this drawing was found on another student at Oyster Harbor Academy, just one day before the body was found in the forest. Despite this, no arrest has been made yet. Guardian Vahreld of the Royal Guardians of Coniston has released a statement saying - "

The TV suddenly turns black, and I jerk my head. My mom's holding the remote, and her hand is shaking.

"I know this looks bad, but I promise you - "

She pulls me in for a tight hug, and her hands dig into my shoulder blades. The heat from her body burns against me and I try to break from her grasp.

"I know you didn't do this. I know, honey. You are a good person. You couldn't have done something like this."

I pull out of the hug and glance over at the clock.

"It's getting late. I've got to get going, otherwise I'll be late."

"Are you sure you want to go to school today? I think you should stay here. At least for today. Or maybe even for the rest of the week?"

"I'll be fine. Don't worry."

As I walk out the front door, she calls out from behind me.

"Be careful Shion!"

Since the Royal Guardians have placed guards throughout the forest and blocked off most of the pathway, there's no choice but to take the neighborhood streets.

I could try to sneak through, but I don't want to take the risk.

As I walk by one of the neighbor's homes, I can see them looking at me through the window. I hold my hand up to wave at them, but then they pull the blinds shut.

One couple turns the corner and is about to walk towards me when they notice me. They turn and walk down the opposite street.

Seems like lots of people saw the news already.

When I pass by Ariy's house, she's already closing the metal gate of the fence surrounding her house. The fence used to surround a lush garden. But now, it only fences dry cracked dirt.

She smiles at me and waves excitedly.

"At least you're not afraid to be with me."

"Of course not. Why would I be afraid of you? I know you didn't do this. And even if you did, that just means you're more powerful to be around. Safer for me, right?"

I snort out a laugh.

She grabs me by the hand, pulling me down a street in the opposite direction of the academy.

"Where are we going?"

"We don't need to go to school today; let's go somewhere else. How about that new cafe? The one that just opened up?"

Mom probably wouldn't like that if she found out. But what could she do?

"Wait, aren't you worried about the scholarship? Ditching school like this is probably going to hurt your chances for the scholarship, right?"

She has a wide grin on her face, enough that her eyes nearly close. "You remember Saho, right? She was the only one close to getting the scholarship, and Fasmoh told me they just disqualified her application this morning! She doesn't know why, but apparently something happened that involved the Royal Guardians."

Once we step into the door of the cafe, I take a deep breath. The scent of freshly ground coffee beans wafts through the air, and I can make out hints of nuts. Much different from the one Mom was using.

Though it's barely 6:30 in the morning, there's already a long line. Most of them are professionally dressed, probably on their way to work.

A loud voice from the front catches our attention.

"Where is the owner? I feel like we haven't seen her here in a while?" The customers in the front of the line asks the cashier.

"I'm sorry. She's not here at the moment. I'm the person in charge today. What can I help you with?"

"Hmm, okay." She finishes placing her order, but stands to the side to continue talking to the employee. "Doesn't she live right above the cafe, though? Have you tried to knock on her door? I haven't seen her recently and wanted to see how she's doing."

The cashier shares a glance with one of the other employees before looking back at the woman and shrugging.

"We tried. She didn't answer. I don't - "

The cashier gets cut off as the woman pushes her way past. "I'm just going to check on her real quick!"

A few of the others try to stop her, but she slips past them.

Ariy digs her nails into my arm. "What do you think is going on? Do you think something happened? Should we go follow her to check it out?"

I shake my head. "No, don't bother. Let's just get our food. We don't want anyone finding out we're here."

I also don't want to do anything else that makes me seem suspicious. Some of the other patrons at the cafe look at me, like they recognize me.

After we place our order, we take one of the open tables close to the back hallway. Even though I didn't want to follow the woman to the second floor, I still want to be nearby in case something happens.

A small cat trots down the hallway, letting out a meow behind my chair. It stops next to our table. It circles my legs a few times before brushing its fur against my leg. Stray orange hairs fly into the air and stick against my leg.

"Aw, how cute! Do you think she came from upstairs?"

I position her between my legs and rub her back as she coughs. After a few dry heaves, she spits out a small hairball onto the table.

Ariy's face twists in disgust, but I ignore it.

"It's okay, you're all right. It was just a hairball." I continue rubbing her back, and she pushes her back into my chest to cuddle against me.

Something in her hairball glistens under the light.

I bend in to look a little closer.

I set the cat aside on the floor and twist my head to inspect the hairball closer.

With a finger, I dig it into the squishy, wet ball and attempt to separate it into smaller pieces. Ariy gags and reaches forward with a napkin to pick it up, but I swat her hand away.

Right in the center of the hairball is a small earring.

Chapter 7

"Why do you always seem to be caught in the middle of these situations?"

Guardian Vahreld uses his boot to drag the chair out from under the table before sitting across from me. "And don't you have classes right now?"

I ignore his questions, and he pulls his hat off to set it on the table. He leans in. He must have had to get ready in a haste, as I can see the patches of his beard that he missed from shaving.

"This isn't looking good for you. I'm trying my best to keep suspicion off of you, but you're not making it easy. You saw the news this morning, right?"

"Yeah."

"I can only protect you for so long." Vahreld casually turns around, before bringing his voice lower to make sure the others can't hear him. "Did you know about this one, too? Is that why you were here?"

My head jerks back, and I squint at him. "What is that supposed to mean?"

"That's your magic, right? You can see into the future?"

I open my mouth, but pause to think about how to respond. His eyes are filled with anticipation.

I might be able to use this to my advantage.

"Yes, you're right. I can see the future. That's how I knew about Arvir and about the cafe owner. But you can't let anyone know."

His mouth widens into a grin. "Even though it seems pretty obvious, I won't tell anyone. I told you before, I want to prove that you're innocent. Did you have a chance to think about the scholarship? I can put a good word in for you. Then you'd be guaranteed to get it."

"No. Thanks, but it's not for me."

"Why not?"

"The Royal Guardians look down on magic. I know what your people do to people like me. I can't be a part of a group that wants to get rid me."

He leans back, and "I understand that. But sometimes you have to work on the inside to help change things. You have the power to enact change. We can do this. Together. If you really want to make things better for people like us, then give it a thought."

Before I can respond, another guard walks over to our table.

"Hey boss. We're done with all the interviews already. Is it time to get going?" The shorter, stockier guard stands beside our table. He eyes me before quickly turning back to Vahreld. "I really want to get home."

"Yeah, let's gather back at the station and then we can call it a night. I know it's been a pretty busy week." He stands up, letting the other man walk away first.

"Think about it, Shion. We need someone like you."

A few minutes later, when the guards let us leave I'm one of the first ones out the door. In my haste to leave, I forget about Ariy.

"What's going on? Is everything all right?" Ariy speeds up to catch up. "I saw that one guard talking to you alone in the back. What did he say? Does he think you're responsible for this?"

"Let's talk about this later, okay? It's getting too late and I really need to get home.."

It took hours for the police to interrogate everyone at the coffee shop. By now, school is long over. I can already imagine my mom's reaction when she realizes I didn't go straight home.

"Wait, slow down! We need to do something. This is the second murder that's happened, and you seem to be caught in the middle of both of them."

I jerk around to face her. "Are you saying that you think I'm the killer?"

She shakes her hand, rubbing her forehead against her palm.

"I'm saying that we need to figure out what's going on. The Royal Guardians suspect you, Shion. They think you're the one behind all of this. Lots of people do. People at the academy, our neighbors. All I want to do is help you. I know you're not responsible for this." She pulls her phone from her pocket, flashing her texts. "I already texted Fasmoh, and she's going to meet us. Come over and we can help you."

"I can't, I need to get home now or my mom's going to get angry at me."

"Then let's go to your place."

I want to protest, but the face Ariy gives me tells me I can't. She has to know how Fasmoh's been feeling about me recently, and I want to keep our friendship intact.

Even if it doesn't mean anything.

I reluctantly agree, and Ariy calls Fasmoh to inform her of the change in plans.

At least I'll have an excuse for why I'm coming home late.

By the time we get to my place, Fasmoh is already sitting on the sidewalk outside of my home, waiting for us.

I unlock the front door, and step inside first to hold the door open for them.

"What are you doing home so late? Where have you - Oh, who are you?" After seeing that I'm not alone, my mom's frown turns into a smile.

"Mom, this is Fasmoh and Ariy. Sorry I'm late. We were hanging out earlier after school ended and didn't notice how late it was. They wanted to stop by to meet you."

Fasmoh waves awkwardly at my mom while Ariy reaches forward to shake hands, a large grin across her face. "Hello, Ms. Kuen. Shion's told us so much about you. I can't believe it's taken this long for us to finally meet."

My mom looks at her before slowly returning the handshake. "Ah, yes of course. It is good to see Shion spending time with friends."

I wonder if the other two can tell she's not happy about my uninvited guests.

"Will they be staying for dinner?"

"No, we're just going to go upstairs for a bit. We have a project that we need to work on for one of our classes. I'll see you later."

I rush them up the stairs to my bedroom, giving them little time for any more conversations. When I look back, she scowls before retreating to the living room.

Once I lock the door behind us, Ariy is already explaining everything that happened at the cafe to Fasmoh.

"I definitely agree with Ariy on this. We need to figure out who the killer is."

"No. This isn't something that we should deal with. Or something that we can deal with. We have to leave this to the guards. They're the only ones that can handle something like this." Even though I'm not following my advice, I don't want to get them involved in this.

"Do you really think the Guard is going to do anything?" When Ariy says this, Fasmoh's face sours.

"They're doing the best they can. The department has a lack of personnel, especially with everything that's been going on in the town. I haven't seen my brother in days because they've been working him overtime."

"A few weeks ago, weren't you the one who said they didn't seem to be doing anything? What's with the change in heart now?"

I can see the tension in Fasmoh's face. I quickly speak up before Ariy can say anything else. "All I'm saying is that this killer is dangerous. Did either of you see what happened to Arvir's body? The person responsible for this is powerful. And dangerous. If we get in their way - ”

“What do you mean you saw his body?”

I freeze, taking a few moments before responding. “Well, I mean his death has been on the news for several days now.”

They share a quick glance before Fasmoh speaks up. “They’ve talked about his death, but not what the crime scene looked like. The police aren’t releasing any descriptions or photos of what happened. That’s what my brother told me at least. I don’t think he even knows what happened.”

“So then how did you see it, Shion?”

I screwed up. I know Vahreld’s been keeping information hidden, but I didn’t know that he was able to hide that much information. With Mom home, I haven’t been able to keep up with the news as much as I wanted to. Every time something about the murders came up, she would immediately turn the TV off or switch it to another channel.

Is he really trying to protect me?

“Look. I don’t really know how to explain it. But sometimes I see things. Things that turn out to happen later on. And recently I’ve been seeing many people we know die in gruesome ways. Classmates, neighbors, family, friends. And I’ve been drawing them, to find out what’s going on.”

“So you’re saying that you have magic?”

Ariy’s face is filled with excitement while Fasmoh looks to be in disbelief.

At least now I only have to keep track of one story. I hope I can keep this up. It's not completely a lie, but it's not the whole truth either.

"I know it might be hard to believe, but it's the truth. Let me show you." I excuse myself and step into my closet, watching their confused faces as I close the door behind me.

In my hideout, Luna is sleeping quietly on one of the steps of the staircase. I smile at him as I pass by. At first I was worried that he would make a lot of noise with the others here, but luckily he's asleep.

I step around his tiny body carefully, and race down the staircase to the center room. Everything is still on the table, just like I left it. Including Arvir's eye.

I pick up the jar, inspecting the eye. My heart starts to race. It looks ready. But I can't do it now, not with them here. I'll have to wait until they're gone.

From one of the shelves, I grab the binder with my drawings and run back up the staircase.

Wait, where's Luna?

I turn to look at the rest of the cavern, trying to see where he went. But he's nowhere in sight.

"Luna?"

I hear a shriek on the other side of the stone wall.

CHAPTER 8

He must have gotten out. I knew I shouldn't have brought them over.

I open the closet door, and Luna is running around the room before jumping up towards Ariy. Ariy seems to enjoy playing with him, but Fasmoh is shrinking away against the wall. Her face is filled with fear before she turns to me. "What is that... thing?"

"That's Luna. He's... kind of my pet, I guess. He was an otter. I guess he still is."

"We have a pet. But our pet has skin."

"So exactly what kind of magic have you been practicing?" Ariy's voice is much more calmed, excited even.

"I've been practicing a bit of necromancy." I quickly add, "I haven't been killing anything, though. Just using dead bodies of animals that I find around. I actually found him in the forest a couple of weeks ago."

"He's so cute! I've never seen one in real life before." Ariy reaches her hand down, pulling it up each time Luna jumps. He's loving the attention.

"So you're a necromancer. Why are you practicing that kind of magic? It's evil, isn't it?" Fasmoh's standing straight with her back against the wall, keeping her distance between herself and Luna.

"I think that the killer is a necromancer. The way that he's been killing people, the ways he mutilates the bodies. I was doing research when I first started having these visions. Most evidence that I came across pointed to necromancy. And I guess I got a little curious. But I haven't killed or hurt anyone. Or anything. I've been trying to learn necromancy ethically."

From how Ariy continues to play with Luna, I can tell she doesn't need any more convincing. Fasmoh still looks at me in disbelief.

"Fasmoh, I promise. I'm not using it to hurt people. I'm only trying to use it to help. Necromancy can help me find who the killer is and stop him."

"Didn't you say that we should leave this alone for the guards to deal with?"

I sigh. "That was to protect the two of you. I don't want either of you to get hurt."

Her face softens, and she watches Ariy and Luna playing. Ariy has Luna held up to her chest, and she pushes him up into the air. He struggles from her grasp before finally resting on her chest.

"Well, it looks like we have to get involved now, doesn't it? To make sure that you don't get hurt, either."

Her words ease my anxiety. I was worried that she was going to turn me in.

"Then let me show you what I know so far." I set down the binder in the center of us, and Ariy sits up, keeping Luna in her lap. He claws at her neck, nuzzling his nose against her. She gives him a kiss, and he curls into her lap.

"These are the deaths that I've been seeing."

They both let out a collective gasp when they open the binder. I open the rings to let them grab handfuls. As they flip through the drawings, Fasmoh points out a few to Ariy. Probably a classmate or professor.

Ariy suddenly freezes, her grip tightening on the piece of paper. "This... is this supposed to be me?" She's struggling to keep her composure, and it looks like she's close to having a breakdown.

"Hey, hey it's going to be alright." Fasmoh leans over to Ariy, pulling her to her side. "We have that protection spell, remember? And you've got us. We won't let anything happen to you. Right, Shion?"

I nod, hiding my clenched jaw behind a smile. I want to tell her everything is going to be okay. But I can't keep lying to them.

Ariy sets her pile down. She crosses her arms, leaning back against the wall. Fasmoh turns back to the pile, picking up a few to examine closer.

"Wait a second. Most of these people, they're from our school, aren't they? Does that mean they're targeting the school for some reason?"

Ariy says, "We can't let this happen, we have to stop it. What are we supposed to do?"

I shift uncomfortably in my seat under the weight of their eyes. I shrug.

"Here's what we're going to do." Fasmoh grabs a few pictures, setting them into different piles on the floor. At first, her pile choices seem random. But she takes a few moments looking at each drawing before setting them into a pile.

Soon, she has three equally stacked piles and hands one to each of us.

"I divided these based on who is most likely to see them during the school day. Some of the people aren't from our school, so I randomly distributed them into each pile. This way, we can try to be on the lookout for any suspicious behavior from anyone. If anything, maybe we can at least figure out who might be next."

Is this really a good idea? Getting them involved in this?

While I don't want the pictures to spread around, if someone finds Ariy or Fasmoh with these pictures, it will at least take the blame off of me.

And at least I won't be the only target if the killer finds out we're investigating.

Before the others leave, we promise to meet in the next few days to discuss any important findings. To my relief, Ariy offers up her place. She says it would be a good time for us to refresh the spells we did last time.

"Definitely going to need more protection after finding out about all of this," Ariy says with a dejected voice.

Once they're gone, I turn to see Mom watching me through the doorway.

"How was your hangout with your friends?"

"It was fine, but I've got some homework. I'll talk to you later."

"What were the three of you doing?" Her question cuts me off before I can go back upstairs.

"I told you earlier, just school stuff."

"Look Shion, I don't know how you know those girls, but I don't think you should be friends with them."

I tilt my head, unsure I heard her correctly.

"What are you talking about? They're my friends."

"I just don't think that they will be a good influence on you. They don't seem... normal." The way my mom is talking right now, I can tell she rehearsed what she was going to say.

"What do you mean by that?"

"Shion! Those girls are not normal. Something is wrong with them. You should hear what some of the other parents from the school say about them. Especially now, with everything going on with your drawing, you need friends that won't bring anymore negative attention to you."

This is what she thinks of my two best friends? The reason we are such good friends is that they were the only ones I could connect to. They were the only ones that didn't ostracize me for being weird.

She reaches a hand out to touch me and I pull away. "Shion, look. I'm just worried about you. If other people think that your friends are involved with these deaths, they might think that you are, too. I don't - "

"Just fuck off, will you? Stay out of my business and stay out of my life."

Her eyes widen and her mouth opens. Her lips move like she's trying to find something to say. Before she can, I sprint my way up the stairs, locking the bedroom door shut.

I can't keep giving her all this attention. I need to figure out who the killer is.

As I'm opening the portal in the closet, the knife shakes in my hand. I gasp as I cut the skin of my palm. A little too deep this time.

I bolt down the staircase, not stopping until I reach the table.

The eyeball floats in the jar. Small pieces of partially dissolved flesh float nearby, clouding the liquid.

I tilt my head back, mentally preparing myself for what I have to do. I inhale a deep breath and hold it for a few seconds before releasing it.

While I'm digging my finger into the jar, the putrid smell of the concoction fills my lungs. My eyes start to tear up.

I finally grip the eye between my thumb and index finger and pull it out.

My own reflection in the eye stares back at me.

With one more deep breath, I close my eyes and stick my tongue out slowly towards the eyeball. The taste of it makes me gag, and I fight the urge to vomit.

Something drags my head backwards, further than normal. My body falls, but it stops before hitting the ground.

I look down to my stomach to see the long black tendril wrapping itself around my body. No matter how hard I struggle against it, it only wraps tighter around my stomach.

The feeling in my body starts to disappear, and all I feel is numbness. I can't even move my body to try to break free.

I watch helplessly as two long tendrils appear from the ceiling above me. They slither in the air for a few seconds before plunging into each of my eyes.

CHAPTER 9

My chest burns. My head is light and I feel dizzy.

After a few gasps, fresh air finally reaches my lungs.

I'm not in my hideout anymore.

Instead of stone walls, I'm surrounded by vast trees. The humid air dampens my skin and clothing.

To the side, a deer freezes in the middle of the clearing. Grass hangs from the side of its mouth. It inspects me, seemingly as confused as I am.

How did I get here?

All of a sudden, the deer drops the grass from its jaw. It sprints away in the opposite direction.

Did I scare it off?

The wind whistles behind me. Ruffling leaves force me to my feet, and I run after the deer.

Something's after me. I don't know who or what it is. But I know that I need to get away from them.

I recognize this forest. I've been here before. This is the same forest in Coniston.

But for some reason, as I run, everything seems different. The same, but different. I recognize some of the older trees, but they appear to be in different spots. As I run down different pathways, the trails all seem slightly off, too.

My foot catches on a rock, sending me rolling forward. Dirt and dust kick up into the air and I cover my face to block out the debris.

I grunt as my back slams against a tree trunk. Pain shoots up my spine from my lower back, and my entire body shudders.

Come on. Get up.

Leaning my weight against the tree trunk, I struggle to steady myself on my feet. My knees buckle as I try to stand, sending me back to the ground.

I can't keep running. There's got to be somewhere I can hide.

There, underneath a nearby tree is a gap. It's small, but it looks big enough to fit my body through.

I limp my way across the ground as quietly as possible. But with every step, the dead leaves crunch under me.

A large tree log is laying on the ground, and dirt covers the top of it. Moss and shrubs surround it, making it a perfect hiding spot.

The small crevice is just large enough for me to drag my body through. I shove myself further into the hole feet first, compressing my body to fit through the rocky surface and trying to keep my body away from the light.

I hide in this position for what feels like hours. My breathing is short and labored. The pressure from above and below my chest makes it hard to take full breaths. Even if I could, I worry that whatever is chasing me might hear me.

Every single noise makes my body jump. Every tree branch snapping, every gust of wind. Goosebumps paint each of my arms.

Finally, the sun is going down. At least it'll be dark enough for me to escape whomever or whatever is chasing me. I never thought I would feel safer in the forest at nighttime, but knowing that I could use the darkness to my advantage eases my fears slightly.

I take a deep breath before pushing myself forward.

The phone in my pocket starts to ring.

I struggle to grab the phone from my pocket. But the space is too small for me to reach down to grab it.

I need to get out first if I want to mute it.

With my body pressed up against the top of my hiding spot, I shimmy my body forward towards the light. A few seconds later, the ringing stops.

My head hangs forward. Thankfully, they hung up.

When I raise my head, a hand is reaching towards me.

It must have heard the ringing.

As quietly as possible, I push my body further back in the hole. My foot hits the back, and a wave of relief washes over me. I'm too far in for them to reach me.

Rather than reaching in further, the hand lifts up with the palm facing me. The light around it fades, as if getting sucked into the hand. Moments later, my entire vision has gone black. There's no dirt, no tree trunk, nothing. There's nothing left but the hand.

The hand warps, wrapping itself around my mouth and ears as I struggle to breathe. Even though I'm far into the hole, it seems to reach me with ease. Soon, the hand spreads, finally covering my entire head before everything goes black.

I struggle to force my eyes open, and when I finally do, I'm back on the hard concrete of the hideout.

Arvir's eye is still in my hand and I bring it back up to my face.

Those must have been Arvir's memories, right until he was killed. It worked! Except it didn't help me at all. He didn't see who the killer was.

Which means I tasted his dead eyeball for no reason.

I guess I'll just have to continue with Ariy's plan. At least until I can obtain more evidence.

As I walk out through the portal, Luna stands on his hind legs, reaching up to me with his front paws. He looks lonely.

"Sorry, but not right now. Next time we can play."

It's getting pretty late and I'm getting hungry, so I open the door to my room. When I step out, my dad is sitting on the floor with his back against the wall. It looks like he's been watching my door for a while for me to come out.

"You're back. That's twice in a week. What's the occasion?" I hope he hears the sarcasm in my voice.

"I hear that you've still been acting strangely. Spending time with the wrong people. Drawing some weird pictures. Locking yourself in your bedroom for long periods of time."

He pauses for a moment, and I wonder how he expects me to respond to that.

Before I can, he continues. "I'm just saying. I don't know what you think you're doing, but whatever it is needs to stop now. You're only making things worse for yourself and your family."

"I'm not the one making things worse for this family. You are. Instead of taking care of us like a normal father, you leave us to fend for ourselves." My chest is starting to tighten, and the words keep spewing from my mouth. "You're not a father. You're not a husband. And you never will be. Why don't you just leave? Don't bother coming back. We're better off without you. We don't want you here."

He looks like he's about to respond, but pauses, looking at the floor. I can't tell if he's trying to make an excuse, or if my comments actually hurt him.

I hope they did hurt him.

"You have no idea what you're talking about. What I sacrificed for this family. What I sacrificed for you."

He turns, resting his hand on the staircase banister. "You won't understand until it's too late."

As he descends the staircase, I call out. "Not staying for dinner again?"

"I have work to do."

Chapter 10

The ball rolls through the open closet door. Luna runs in to chase after it. When he returns, he eagerly drops it at my feet and jumps on his two hind, skeletal legs.

I roll the ball again for him.

This time, after he drops the ball at my feet, he begs for me to pick him up. I lift him, letting his body rest against my chest. I grab his paws, lifting them up and down as I rub my face into his body. He cuddles up to me underneath my arm, and I pull him in tightly.

He looks happy.

For the past few days, I've stayed at home. I haven't gone to school, met up with my friends, or even left the house.

Some days, just getting out of bed seems like a chore. I don't even remember the last time I showered.

Good thing Luna can't smell me.

It's nice seeing him excited to have me home so much. I felt bad about leaving him locked up in the closet whenever I was gone, and this is the first time I've seen him so happy.

Too bad it won't last.

I pull the curtains open and the bright sunlight blinds me. I peek my head through once my vision adjusts to look out.

Outside, Mom is standing on the sidewalk. She turns from side to side, as if she was waiting for someone. After a few minutes, a small car drives up to the street. It's a dark black car with red words on the side of it that say Royal Guardians.

What are they doing here?

Mom runs over to the passenger door of the car, sticking her head in to talk to someone. I wish I could hear what they're talking about.

The car drives away, and I jerk the curtains shut. My room is once again shrouded in darkness.

Why were they here? Are they watching me to make sure nothing happens?

Since I've been home, there haven't been any more murders. I should be happy about that, but I'm not. It just makes me more suspicious. And I haven't found any new evidence to help us figure out who the killer is.

My phone vibrates on my nightstand, and I reach out to grab it.

I hope it's not Ariy or Fasmoh.

Staying at home meant that I made no progress with our investigation. I know the others have been investigating, as they write excited texts in our group chat about their findings. Most of it wasn't helpful. Just a lot of gossip about what our classmates and professors have been doing.

At least neither of them complained that I'm not pulling my weight. Yet.

Hey Shion, how've you been? What are you doing tonight? Ariy asks.

Nothing. There's nothing to do here besides playing with Luna all day. I can't leave the house, at least not for a few more days. My mom wants me to stay at home to make sure that nothing happens and to ease some of the attention on me.

Sneak out. We're going to Wanderlust.

Wanderlust? Why are they going there?

Even though I've lived in Coniston for as long as I can remember, I've never been to Wanderlust before. At least not before it fell. But I always heard stories about it from the other students. It was always rumored to be a place of magic and oddities.

Which is also why my mom would never let me go. Especially not now.

I can't. My mom's home. She'll find out if I leave.

Just meet us up once she falls asleep. We're going to stay for the whole night. We found a break in the case that we need to talk to you about.

A break in the case? Why would they be at Wanderlust for the case? Did something happen there? Was the killer in Wanderlust?

All right, I'll meet you there around 10:00.

Once it's near 9:00, Footsteps make their way upstairs from the bottom floor. I wait a few more minutes before peeking my head out my door. Her light is already off.

I rap my fingers against the wood, loud enough that she could hear it if she were awake. No response.

I push the door open, trying to sneak a peek. The blankets covering her body rise up and down, but she doesn't move otherwise.

I pause at my dad's door, trying to figure out if I should even bother to check on him. He's probably not even home. And even if he was, I don't want to talk to him.

Since our last interaction, I haven't seen him again. I wonder if it's because of what I said to him or if he's just been busy. Either way, I'm glad.

My hand rests on the doorknob. If he is there, do I really want to see him?

Even my mom didn't want me going in there. When I was younger, I was curious about what he was doing. I never saw him. And I missed him. By the time I had turned the doorknob, Mom was already out of her room, slamming the door shut and yelling at me.

That night was the hardest she ever hit me.

I shake the memories from my head before pulling my hand away from the doorknob. Even if he is here, I don't care. It's not like he's going to tell Mom that I left. And I'll be back in time before she wakes up.

The walk to Wanderlust takes an hour using the forest trail. Even though the forest is still sectioned off, none of the guards are there.

Not surprising. This week has been the most they've worked in years.

When I step out of the woods, the bright lights and vivid colors draw my attention.

From afar, the sidewalks cross above and below each other, and I notice that some buildings have pathways leading from the main street directly to higher floors. None of the layout of the town seems to follow any structure.

Even the buildings are unique, unlike any other buildings I've ever seen before in my life. They're all different sizes, shapes, colors. Some tower over the others, while several are tall enough for people to stand in.

One building near the entrance is adorned with flashing lights that alternate to form distinct patterns.

As I approach the gates of Wanderlust, I notice the smaller details that I couldn't see from the pathway.

Overflowing garbage bins line the road, creating mounds of trash around them. A man drops a cup on top of the garbage, and it bounces a few times before rolling away on the ground. The streets and sidewalks are stained a dark brown color.

Once I pass through the town gate, all I can smell is the scent of feces and urine mixed with rotting meat. I can't tell if that's from their food or from something else.

If they supposedly have so much magic here, why do they live in such filth?

I search for street signs or some kind of map. Which way am I supposed to go? The streets don't seem to follow any patterns. Instead of parallel roads, each sidewalk seems to zig-zag in random directions.

With nothing to guide me, I send a quick text to the group message. There's no immediate response, so I decide to take the street down to my left. The town didn't seem too big from the outside. Hopefully, I'll catch up with them soon.

Some shops have signs with what they're selling, but many others have no identifying features. One window has wooden boards nailed across it. I wonder if people live there.

A lone building catches my eye.

This one is much smaller than the rest, but it has a tent flap propped up over the sidewalk to extend its area. Smoke from inside wafts its way into the street.

Inside, two people are sitting across from each other. Their heads tilt up to the ceiling.

As I walk closer, the man's head jerks forward. His eyes are wild and he swings his head from side to side before turning to the woman in front of him. It's Mr. Ikontye. What's he doing here?

"Please, please I need to go back again!" He begs, voice cracking.

"Your session is over. If you are looking to go back, then you must return next week."

"I can't wait until next week! Please, it will be quick. I'll pay again! I'll pay you more this time!" He reaches into his pocket to pull his wallet out.

"I cannot. Those are the rules."

"No! You can't keep me from them!" When he stands, the table between them almost topples over, and the woman grabs it to steady it.

He grabs at the table, trying to pull it from her grasp. She jerks it away, swiping it from his hands.

"Please, I'm begging you. I need to go back. I need to make things right with them. If I can just try once more, everything will be okay. I was so close, so close. I know what I have to do now."

She crosses her arms in front of her, letting her head fall forward as she shakes her head. "I am sorry."

Mr. Ikontye stands there for a few seconds, face filled with desperation. After seeing that she won't budge, his shoulders slump and he walks away from the tent. He doesn't even notice me as he brushes past me.

"Are you okay?"

When I turn to the woman, I can see her more clearly. It's Kalansa. She looks exactly how I remember her, but younger. Her once thin and gray hair is now in luscious white curls that spread down and out from her face. The liver spots that once dotted her body are gone.

She recognizes me. Her face widens in surprise before she closes her eyes.

I shouldn't have come here.

"Ah, I suspected that something like this was going to happen. You seek me out. You are ready to return, then?"

"I - I'm just going to meet some friends."

She looks confused. "You are not here to see me?"

"Not yet. But soon, I promise."

Her smile turns into a frown. "What do you mean you are not ready? You are only supposed to come see me once you are ready to go back. Were you not told of the rules?"

"I... I'm sorry. I didn't mean to come here. I was just walking by and you were in trouble and I thought you needed help."

"You didn't mean to? How could you not mean to? You were explicitly told not to come here unless you needed to return. Don't you know what you've done?"

A few people in the streets have stopped to turn to us, and I slip into the gap between them. Even though the streets are bustling, I can still make out her yells through the crowd.

"You need to return immediately. You are not welcome in this place!"

I really, really shouldn't have come here. I knew Kalansa would be here, and I knew I wasn't supposed to be. But it's too late now, I've already done it. Hopefully, everything will be fine.

I pull out my phone, surprised to see that I missed several texts.

Did your mom catch you?

I quickly type out a response, noticing that it's been several minutes since Fasmoh last sent a message.

Sorry, got delayed. Here now. Where should we meet?

Come on, we're at the reflecting pools right now. Near the restaurants.

I've never been to the reflecting pools before, so I take a while to find it. When I do, I see Fasmoh standing near the entrance. Bright flashing lights on the building behind her spell out The Hall of Reflecting Pools.

Next to her is a long line of people waiting to enter.

"What took you so long?"

The line has gotten even longer by the time we stand at the end. I look around the corner, tapping my foot.

"So what's going on? Why did you need me to come here tonight? Ariy said the two of you had some sort of lead?"

"We were looking for any help that we could find, and someone sent us a message on an online forum. The same one we used to find those spells. They said that something similar happened in their town, and they had some information that could help us."

"And they told you to meet them up here? Why here, of all places? Why not a coffee shop?"

She shrugs.

"Did they say who they were?"

"Yeah, it was Jarad Duman."

Jarad?

Why do I recognize that name? He can't be from our school; she said he was from a different town. But why does his name sound so familiar?

By the time we're close to the front of the line, I'm still trying to figure out where I recognize that name from.

Then it hits me. My chest tightens, and I struggle to breathe. My body feels numb, and I steady myself against the wall.

Fasmoh reaches to touch me, concern filling her face.

I brush up against the customer in front of me, ignoring her complaints as I address the man sitting in front of the entrance. "Hey, excuse me? Do you know how much longer until we can go inside?"

The employee glances up from his phone to look at me before looking back down. "I get a text when they want me to send the next group in. They haven't texted me yet."

Every moment that passes by makes my heart pound harder.

"Shion, are you okay?"

"Yeah, yeah, don't worry. But we need to get inside now."

I turn back to the employee. "Hey, they haven't texted still? It's been several minutes, and the line is getting really long."

He holds his phone up to me, showing me the last text.

Last group is still inside. Maybe they got lost?

I shove my way past the couple in front of us, grabbing Fasmoh by the hand and ducking under the belt blocking the entrance. Both of them protest, and the employee tries to position himself between us and the door.

"Hey, you can't - "

"Sorry! We'll be quick. It's an emergency."

Before he can stop us, we're already inside the building. I half expect him to follow us, but he doesn't.

"What's going on? Why are you in such a hurry?"

"Jarad is already dead."

CHAPTER 11

"What do you mean, he's already dead? How do you know?" She pauses before asking a final question. "Who's Jarad?"

"I did some research the past few days, and before the murders started here, similar murders happened in Eahmore. A few hours south of us. Violent and gruesome murders that were never solved, just like the ones that have been happening here."

"What does that have to do with us? And Jarad?"

"Jarad was one of the victims."

She falls silent, and I pull her through the door at the end of the hallway.

No one else is here. Besides the small well of water in the center of the room surrounded by red brick blocks, it's empty.

I step closer, looking into the glistening water. It has to be shallow. But no matter how hard I try, I can't seem to see the bottom.

"Whoever is contacting you must be impersonating Jarad. How long have you two been in contact with him?"

"Uhm, I think it's been about 2 or 3 days. He told us to come meet him here and when we got here, we didn't hear from him. We figured he lost service in here."

"So Ariy went in to search for him? Alone?"

She nods. "If we find the person behind the texts, that must be the killer, then, right?"

I ignore her question, and pace the room, trying to figure out where to go. But there's nothing here besides the pool of water.

"You've never been here before, have you?"

I shake my head.

Fasmoh steps up to the edge of the pool and looks through it.

"It's a reflecting pool. We watch the reflections. Sometimes the reflections show something different that isn't here. When you see something that you think is what you're looking for, that's when you go. But if you take too long and it passes, then you miss your chance. You have to wait for it to come back."

She sees the confusion and worry on my face. "It's like one of those mirror mazes, but more difficult and frustrating."

"And people enjoy this?"

We stand around the pool, watching the still waters. For several seconds, all I see are our faces.

"Look!"

Something is in the water, above Fasmoh's head. It looks like a crack forming on the wall. It spreads along the entire wall.

When we turn, there's nothing there.

"Ready?"

The surface of it doesn't feel wet. Instead, it feels... soft. As I press down, it cushions my entire arm. Then the rest of my body.

I'm falling head first. Away from the surface.

I reach to grab at the room, but it drifts further and further away.

Soon it's gone. I turn, seeing bright blue waters all around us. I reach my hand to touch one of the fish, but the water avoids my body and the fish splits in two, swimming on either side of my arm.

I continue to fall through the water, closing my eyes and deepening my breaths. I could fall asleep.

Air brushes the top of my head, and the softness disappears. My body tenses.

We're sitting in a new room. Similar to the last one, but with more pools of water. And people.

"Fasmoh? Shion?" I notice Ariy stepping towards us. I recognize Relli and others from the school huddled in groups behind her. None of them appear happy to see us. "How did you find us?" Ariy asks again.

Fasmoh answers for us. "We came through the first pool. Why are you waiting here? Did something happen?"

"I don't know what's going on, but every path we take, no matter how different it is each time. It always leads us back here somehow. I've gone through dozens of different pathways."

Fasmoh asks "How is that possible? It shouldn't be too hard. We've already done this several times before. None of you have been able to figure out how to get out?"

Before Ariy can answer, one of Relli's friends hyperventilates. She falls to the floor, leaning her back against the wall and tilting her head to the ceiling. Relli sits beside her, squeezing her hand a few times to help calm her.

It doesn't work.

"We gotta get out of here. I can't take this any longer! I can't even remember how long we've been in here. It feels like we've been stuck here for days!"

Relli pulls out their phone, showing the screen to their friend. "Hey, it's okay. I set a timer. It's only been 15 minutes so far. Don't worry. That's just part of the attraction. It can make you go crazy. Don't worry, they always have a timer. If someone can't get out, they'll turn off the magic."

Her eyes glaze over in a daze. "Are we going to die here? Like Arvir?"

A small voice crackles on the speakers. "Reflecting Pool customers, thank you for your patronage at our attraction today. Please exit through this pool to return to the entrance. We have rerouted it to take you back to the front. Please exit one by one in a prompt manner."

Right as she says this, the pool on our left turns a deeper blue color. Arrows on the floor light up along the pathway, directing us to the pool.

The others start to hurry to the exit. Relli grabs their friend and guides her to the others.

Ariy turns. "I guess we won't be finding - "

Her voice cuts off, and blood hits me in the face. I wipe at my eyes, trying to see what's happening.

A long black tendril emerges from her neck. Blood drips from the edge.

Her head cracks and raises, and blood flows from her mouth.

More tendrils of darkness emerge from the pool behind her, stabbing her through the body several times. Through her legs, her arms, her stomach.

"Ariy!"

"Shion…" Her voice trails off as she's dragged backwards into the pool. One of her arms reaches out leaving a bloody handprint on the side of the pool as she disappears.

"Ariy!" Fasmoh runs forward, reaching towards the pool that took away our friend.

"Fasmoh, wait! It's too dangerous!"

The tendrils reach back through the pool, flying outward and digging themselves into the walls and floor. It rips apart. Cracks appear on the floor and walls, revealing oceans of roaring red waves.

"Watch out!"

Relli leaps forward, shoving her away just in time as the floor gives out beneath her. Fasmoh's body slumps against the opposite wall.

They hang from the edge of the ground, struggling to pull their body weight. The red water reaches towards their ankles.

The concrete holding them up cracks, dropping them into the waters below. I grit my teeth, turning back in Fasmoh's direction.

"Fasmoh, stay there! I'll try to get to you."

The floor beneath my foot gives, and I jump off to grab the side of one pool.

"Shion!"

She presses her back against the wall. The surrounding floor is gone, leaving only a tiny piece of broken platform to hold her.

"Jump over to me and grab my arm!"

She looks at the ground, shuffling back as debris falls from her edge.

"Fasmoh, you have to do it now, please!"

The rest of the floor gives underneath her weight and her yell fills the room.

Fuck!

Her fingers grasp against mine, and the extra weight pulls me. My sweaty hand starts to slip from the bricks.

"Don't let go! I'm going to pull us up!"

"Please, please hurry!"

I struggle to gather the strength to pull us up. My elbow almost reaches the floor before it slips.

Her hand breaks away from mine, and the red water wraps around her body, pulling her down into its depths.

I swing my other arm to grab the edge of the pool. I'm barely able to lift my chest up to the edge. Before I push myself up, I turn back to the water.

The waves crash against the sides of the walls, breaking off more pieces of concrete into the water.

It's too thick to see anything. No signs of Fasmoh or Relli.

I take a breath before letting my body fall into the water.

CHAPTER 12

The cold water engulfs my body. The heavy pressure nearly crushes me.

A touch on my shoulder startles me.

"What's going on?" When I lift my head off the ground, I see Relli and Fasmoh standing around me. "Where are we?"

The bright white wallpaper of the building is gone. Instead, textured cave walls surround us. Drops of water fall from the ceiling, plopping against the rocky floor.

Relli's the first to respond. "After I fell through, I woke up here. I thought I died. But the two of you appeared after. What is this place?"

Fasmoh walks around, pacing the rest of the room and inspecting the walls. She slaps her palm against it. "It feels like a cave. Do you think we fell through the floor straight into the ground?"

But there's no hole or break in the ceiling. Just jagged rocks hanging down.

"The red waters must have been a portal that took us here." I point to the winding staircase in the corner of the room. "It looks like that's the only way for us to go if we want to get out of here."

Relli glares at me for a few moments. "I'm supposed to follow the two of you? How do I know you aren't the ones behind all of this?"

"I was actually talking to Fasmoh. You don't have to do anything. If you don't trust us, you're welcome to find your own way out of here."

They look down at the ground, shuffling their feet below them. Defeat crosses their face. "Fine, but just because we have to work together, doesn't mean I trust you."

The three of us take the winding staircase. Fasmoh takes the front, taking each step carefully.

At the top, a short hallway made of wooden planks nailed together leads to a pair of doors. On either side are two tables, various tools scattered on top. I recognize a few of them, but most of them look much more complex than anything I've seen before.

Some of them appear to have been used recently.

"What... what is that? Isn't that Ariy's?" Fasmoh reaches forward to grab the necklace on the table.

"Fasmoh! Wait!"

But my warning comes too late. As her hand approaches the gold chain, a small ball of blue stops her hand. Her finger tip touches it before she can pull away.

She gasps and holds her hand up to her face. She inspects it, but she doesn't scream or anything. "What was that? It doesn't hurt or anything."

"It looks fine. Does it feel okay?" Fasmoh nods in response to Relli's question. But when I take a quicker look, something looks wrong. The blue color of the ball is now on the tip of her finger.

I need to move fast.

Against her protests, I grab her by the hand and slam it down on the table.

"Shion, what are you doing?"

I hold my hand above hers and summon a small silver blade in my hand. Relli tries to grab my arm, but I shove them away, down to the floor.

I slice the blade across her wrist, severing her hand from the rest of her arm in one quick swipe.

As the blade passes through her hand, it steams, burning the flesh and skin around it.

She yells, voice filled with pain and anger. Pulling away from me, she stares at me with bewildered eyes. Relli pulls her behind them and steps in between the two of us.

"Are you okay, Fasmoh?" They turn towards me before continuing. "I knew it! I knew something was wrong with you. I knew we couldn't trust you."

It takes them a while to look at where I'm pointing.

"I had to."

The tip of her severed finger twitches. The tiny blue dot pulses, before expanding and spreading through her whole hand. Seconds later, the entire hand is blue. It rocks violently on the table before the blue disappears. Her hand vanishes.

"What... what was that? What did you do to me?" Fasmoh inspects her wrist where her hand used to be, turning it from side to side.

"That was from whatever spell the killer placed on Ariy's necklace. It was some curse or something like that. All I did was cut your hand off, so it didn't spread to the rest of your body."

Fasmoh stands, inspecting the rest of her body. She looks one more time at her missing hand.

"It's an enchanted blade. That's why you don't feel as much pain as you should have. And now you don't have to worry about it getting infected."

"So you do have magic?" Relli asks, still sitting on the floor.

"Yeah, I do. If that's going to be a problem for you, then like I said before, you're welcome to find your own way out of here."

"No, I didn't mean it like that. It's not a problem for me, really. I didn't expect you to have magic. I didn't expect anyone to have magic. It always used to be fairy tales, something I heard people talk about happening to others. I never thought it could be real."

"Do you still think I'm the one who killed Arvir?"

They pause for a moment before shaking their head.

"Let's go. We need to find a way out of here."

Before we open the doors, I take a quick glance over at the other table.

Are those bones?

"So, when did you find out you had magic?" Fasmoh's voice is a whisper.

I shrug.

She grabs me by the arm, turning me to face her.

"Shion, we've known each other for pretty much our entire lives. We've been friends for years. I always felt like I knew everything about you. Then you changed. One day, you started acting weirdly. You talked differently, you acted differently. And you stopped caring. About me, about Ariy, about anything."

Relli looks uncomfortable and turns away from us.

"I'm the same person I've always been."

"No, you aren't."

"Uhm, sorry to interrupt, but she's kind of right. You've been acting differently this year. Honestly, we were scared of you. That's why Arvir got so mad when he saw that drawing you made, because he thought you were threatening to kill him or something. Especially with all the stories about what's been going on in the rest of the world."

Both of them look at me.

"Look, I told you pretty much everything. I found out I had magic, and I started to learn how to use it. Maybe that's why I've been acting so differently. Don't you think that would make you change?"

"Of course it would. But not in the way you changed."

I let out a loud groan before turning to the door at the opposite end of the room.

"We can waste our time here talking about this, or we can find our way out. Your choice."

CHAPTER 13

The next room is different. We're not in the cave anymore. Instead, it resembles the hallway of a hotel.

The floor is now a soft, red carpet, and a line of dim lights illuminates the pathway. No matter how hard I try, I can't seem to see the end. On each side, tall red doors continue forever down the hall. All of them are identical, with no markings to differentiate between them.

"Where do we go now?" Fasmoh asks.

They both turn to me, as if waiting for instructions.

Do they think that just because I have some magic that I know how to get out of every magical situation?

"Just be careful and watch out for anything weird or unusual."

We spread out to investigate different doors. I stop in front of one to the right. Before opening it, I run my hand over the doorknob and on the surrounding wall.

It seems safe.

I pull it open. Inside is only darkness. There's nothing in the room but darkness. No walls, no ceiling, no floor.

I want to stick my hand through it, but decide against it. I don't know what would happen.

"Here!" Relli yells out to us. They're motioning into an open doorway.

On the other side is the front entrance. It looks like we're watching from the front doors of the building. There are flashing lights of the Royal Guardians' cars and ambulances. Several people from earlier are outside, talking to the guards and the paramedics.

But no one seems to notice us. Even the few that are looking towards the entrance don't seem to be phased at all by us.

Can they see us?

Before either of us can stop them, Relli puts their foot through the doorway.

Fasmoh steps forward and I grip her by the arm. "Shion, come on. We have to leave."

But something's wrong. I can't let her go.

The door is wide open, and Relli steps onto the sidewalk. Once they do, the people outside turn. Several guards take a step towards Relli.

"Hurry, what if something…"

Fasmoh's sentence trails off. Everyone outside is now on their feet. They all look happy. All at once, they clap.

Relli takes a step backwards, looking at the bright, excited faces around them. Their back hits the doorway, unable to pass through.

A few people in the back of the crowd step forward. One of them accidentally steps on another person's foot, sending her falling down to the floor.

But they don't stop.

The people behind the fallen woman continue to step forward, stepping onto her back and her legs. Her body spasms, but they continue to walk. More of them fall, landing on top of her and creating a small pile.

One man I recognize from school falls on the pile. With the smile still painted on his face, he attempts to stand, lifting an arm to drag himself up.

His arm has melded with the rest of the people below him. As he raises an arm, the skin connects it to the person underneath him, stretching. More people fall on top, adding on to the human abomination. Arms and legs reach out, dragging the pile forward.

Relli falls back against the doorway. They turn back to us, hand up against the invisible barrier. Their mouth opens and closes rapidly. It looks like Relli is trying to beg for help, but we can't hear anything.

"We can't do anything for them now. It's too late."

Fasmoh's eyes are wide, and her mouth falls open. She turns back to the door, unsure of what to do.

The mass of bodies drags itself closer. By now, Relli is the last single person. All they can do is press themselves against the doorway, shrinking away from the creature.

A limb of bodies rises. I kick the door shut and Fasmoh falls to her knees.

"We have to help them. We have to." She's crying into her arms.

"There's nothing we can do. They're gone."

When she turns to me, her eyes narrow. The muscles in her face tense.

"What do you mean, we can't do anything? What is wrong with you? Ariy's dead, and now Relli is in trouble. Why are you acting so heartless?"

I pull her body into mine. "I'm so sorry." If only I could tell her everything, to make her understand.

But I can't. It would only make everything worse.

There's a small creaking sound, and I squint my eyes at the door.

"Did you hear that?"

Fasmoh shakes her head. "What?"

The door creaks again, louder this time. The wood bends before snapping. Through the hole, we can see the creature.

The faces of the people continue to smile as the creature shoves their bodies through the gap in the door. Flesh rips off. Several of the limbs bend the wrong way.

I have never seen something like this. This is what necromancy is?

The rest of the door splinters, breaking apart on the floor.

I feel an arm grabbing my collar. Fasmoh drags me backwards.

We take one look back at the creature crawling its way towards us. As each limb slaps against the carpet, it lets out a wet, slopping noise. It's slow, but the body takes up the entire width of the hallway.

It's the last thing I see before Fasmoh pulls me into the darkness.

Chapter 14

Where's Fasmoh?

I can't feel her hand in mine.

When I try to call out for her, no sound comes.

There's nothing.

I try to lift each leg to take steps forward. But I can't even feel my legs or the floor. Am I even moving? I reach out with my hands, but there's still nothing.

"Tell me, why are you looking for me?" A voice rings through my ears. The voice is deep. Is it a man's voice? It sounds like it, but I can't tell for sure.

It's coming from everywhere around me. I try to turn in circles. But there's no one.

My voice sounds. "I am looking for the one responsible for the murders here in Coniston. If that is you, then you are the one I'm looking for."

"And what did you expect to happen when you found me?"

I pause, pondering the voice's question.

"To find out how you've been doing all of this. To put an end to your terror and save the people of Coniston."

The voice laughs, the sound booming in my ears. "My terror? I've only killed those that were necessary. I'm not the one your town needs saving from."

Before I can ask what he means, he continues. "I've been watching you. You are powerful, much more powerful than the rest of the people in your town. Tell me, do you think you are powerful enough to stand against me?"

"I do not know."

"Yet you still wish to face me?"

He notices my hesitation.

I respond. "I will do whatever I can to protect the ones I love."

"You're just like the others. Looking for an answer to all your problems. For a right and a wrong. Someone to blame. But it's not that simple, Shion."

He says my voice with confidence. How did he know my name?

"You cannot imagine what is to come. This is bigger than you, your friends, and your town. Take this as your last warning. Give up before it's too late for you."

The voice fades away, leaving me with one last thought. "Be careful with whom you trust."

It's gone now. The darkness around me swirls, and the black around me melts away.

"Shion? Shion!"

Fasmoh's voice snaps me to consciousness.

We're back at the beginning again. The pool that we first went through sits in the middle of the room, right next to where I lay.

I rub my temples and close my eyes. My head is pounding and I can barely focus.

"What... what happened? Where did he go? I heard his voice. He was talking to me, Fasmoh. The killer. Did you hear him too?"

Her eyes are wide, and she shakes her head. Small strands of her bright orange hair poke out from under her khimar.

"Just hurry and get up, please. We'll talk about it once we're free from this place."

I let her pull me by the wrist and drag me out through the front doors. After what felt like hours, we're back at the entrance where everything started.

Guardian Vahreld sees us and shoves his way through the crowds of people to reach us. He grabs us by the hands, guiding us to an empty ambulance on the side of the building.

"Are you two okay? What happened in there? Why did it take you so long to get out?"

I let Fasmoh take over explaining what happened. She describes both Ariy's and Relli's deaths to him. When she gets to the room of darkness, she mentions nothing about the voice.

Does that mean she didn't hear it?

"And both of your friends, they're still in there?"

We nod. His eyes close, and he drops his head forward.

When he notices her hand, she reaches it forward to let him look it over. "What happened here?"

Fasmoh glances at me before responding. "Uh, well, we got attacked inside and some creature ripped my hand off."

He looks at it for a few seconds. The part of her wrist where I cut her hand off is completely healed over. He pokes it gently.

"Is it okay? Is there any pain or anything?"

"It just disappeared. No pain, no blood." Her head falls forward. "Is Jhakan here? My brother? Dad said he was working late tonight."

"No, I'm sorry. He's doing rounds at Coniston. They kept several of us back in case something happened while we were gone." Vahreld rests his hand on Fasmoh's shoulder. "But we will search for as long as we can to find your friends."

"Fasmoh? Let me through!" A shorter man in a chair maneuvers his way past the others, stopping in front of Fasmoh. He pulls her into his chest, rubbing her back with his hands as she sobs into his shoulder.

I wish I had someone that cared for me like that.

A tapping on my shoulder causes me to jump. Vahreld motions for me to join him on the side of the ambulance. When we're out of sight from the others, he leans against the passenger door, arms crossed.

"Can you tell me what happened in there?"

I still don't know if I should trust him, but right now, he's the only one I can talk to.

"I talked to the killer. At least I think I did. I didn't see him. I could only hear his voice."

"Did you find out any information? Who he is? How he's been doing all of this?"

I shake my head and lower my gaze to the floor. None of what the killer was saying made sense. Who shouldn't I trust?

"It's okay, Shion. You did well. I'm sorry about your friends, but this just means we're one step closer to figuring out who's behind all of this. We're going to find the person responsible for this. Don't worry."

"Shion!" A familiar voice shouts over the other voices.

No, not right now. Please.

Her piercing stare causes me to shrink back against the ambulance. But it's too late. She's already seen me.

I see Mom shove her way through two Royal Guardians, almost knocking one of them over. The other looks like she's about to reach for her gun, but Vahreld holds his hand up to her.

"Hin, thank you for coming."

"What's going on here? What happened?" She grabs my face in between her hands, turning my head from side to side before holding my head forward. "Why didn't you stay at home like I told you to? None of this would have happened if you just listened to me. I told you that you were never to come here!"

"Mom. It's fine. I'm fine. Stop worrying."

She raises her voice louder, and others around us turn to look. "Why are the guards here? Don't you know how this looks? Every single time something bad happens, you always are right in the middle of it all? Why can't you just listen to me?"

This isn't fair. Fasmoh's dad comforts her and tries to make her feel better, and all my mom can do is yell at me? Blame me for what's happening, when all I'm doing is trying to help. I'm just trying to find out who's hurting our people.

But she doesn't care.

"I'm an adult. You have no control over me or what I choose to do. My friends were in trouble, and they needed me to help them. One of them is dead. The other barely survived. If I wasn't there for them, who knows what would have happened? They needed me, can't you understand that?"

"I don't care about your friends, and I don't care about anyone else. You - "

"Thats because you're a fucking horrible person!"

Everyone around us has stopped their conversations. All of their eyes are on us.

Vahreld steps forward between us, holding both his hands up. "I think right now, with the rough night that he has had, Shion just really needs to be at home. Safe. I know there are a lot of feelings right now, but this isn't the time for it. Please, take him home. Take care of him."

She opens her mouth before letting it close.

"Let's go."

CHAPTER 15

L una rubs against my arm before he leans back onto his hind legs. He swipes at my arm playfully.

I groan and tilt my body. He shoves his head into the gap, resting his head on my chest. My arm drops behind him, and I hug him.

My stomach is gnawing away at itself again. It growls, shaking Luna from his quick nap.

What time is it? I've been awake for hours, but I didn't have the strength to pull myself out of bed. It's got to be past lunch time at least.

Before I can reach my phone, there's a knocking on the door. I jump from my bed, rushing Luna back into the closet. Sadness covers his face.

Sorry, buddy. I can't let her find you.

Satisfied that he won't be able to get out, I lean against the door. "Yeah?"

"I wanted to check up on you. You haven't eaten all day." She turns the doorknob, trying to get the door open. The lock holds it in place.

"I'm not hungry."

My stomach growls. Loudly enough that I know she can hear it.

"Why don't we go somewhere to eat? There's a restaurant between here and Eahmore. Unless you're not hungry."

"Yeah, fine. I'll be out soon."

"I need to get ready, too. We can leave in a few minutes."

I keep my body pressed against the door until her footsteps disappear.

It's been a long time since we've gone out to eat together.

Is Dad coming? I'm tempted to ask, but decide against it. I don't want him to come. By the time I meet her at the car, it's still just the two of us. I notice the indentation in my bottom lip from where I was biting down on.

We sit in silence for most of the car ride. Thirty minutes later, we pull up to a restaurant. The Mystic Champagne.

"It has pretty good reviews. I hope you like it."

"Yeah, sure."

We're seated right as we walk into the restaurant. It's empty. I see only two other groups of people, and one of them looks like they're about to leave.

Mom orders a few drinks first, and the waiter brings it out. The food still hasn't come out, and Mom's already tipsy.

"You all right to drive?"

"Yeah, yeah, of course!" Her head moves back and forward, and her eyes look lazily back at mine.

I swipe her keys from her side, and it takes a second for her to notice.

"I'll drive."

She laughs before grabbing the wine glass. In a few gulps, it's empty again.

We sit in silence, only interrupted when she asks the waiter for another glass. He already has one in his hand.

"About yesterday..." she starts, but her voice trails off.

"It's fine."

"Look, I'm worried, Shion. About you. I just want to protect you and keep you safe. Sorry if sometimes it's... controlling."

I press my lips together. "It's okay. I should have told you where I was going."

She reaches her hands out to grab mine, holding them tight into her grasp. "I'm sorry, I will try to do better. With just the two of us... we can't keep fighting like this. This can't be the relationship we have. I know I shouldn't have gotten mad at you last night, but I was scared. When I got the call..."

This is the most of an apology I ever heard from her. In my entire life.

My chest opens up and my body feels lighter. The tension in my back disappears, and I shrink back into the seat.

"I'm sorry about dad."

Her chest deflates.

"I miss him. And sometimes I forget you must miss him, too. It's been hard on me. Sometimes I can't see how hard it can be on you, too."

Tears pour from her eyes, and her body shakes. Before I know it, she knocks her glass off the table and it shatters on the floor.

"Mom!"

Our waiter steps toward her, but she holds a hand out. "I'm so sorry, don't worry about this. I'll clean it up."

I stop her from bending over. If she picks up the pieces of glass like this, she might cut herself.

"I'm so sorry about her, she's had too much to drink. Let me take her to the car."

When we get inside, I pull the seat belt across her chest. The lock clicks. She hangs her head forward, eyes closed.

"Home. Please."

The wheel shakes in my hand as I reverse. I haven't driven in a long time. When I pull out of the rocky driveway, the smoothness of the main road eases some of my fears.

She tilts her head back and laughs.

"What's going on? Are you okay?" I want to turn to turn to her, but I can barely see the road through the darkness.

Her laugh dies down, and she speaks. "Great job back there."

"What do you mean?"

"On getting us out of there. You didn't pay the bill, did you?"

I realize we just left. No one paid for the drinks.

My head heats up, and realization hits me. "You did all of that just to skip out on the bill? Pretending to be sad and knocking over the glass? Why would you do something like that?"

"What did you expect me to do, Shion? Pay for it?" She huffs out a breath of air. "Well, surprise. We're running out of money."

"Running out of money? How? Isn't your job still paying you on your days off?"

Her head shakes back and forward, and she looks up to the ceiling. "Shion, there is no job. Not anymore. Come on, Shion. Did you really think the hospital could afford to give me days off? And pay me? They fired me. They fired me when they found out that you were being investigated for the murders."

She told me she took those days off to keep a close eye on me.

"This is all dad's fault, isn't it?"

She pauses. "What? What do you mean by that?"

"All of this. The reason you have to work so much. What is he doing every day? Why isn't he working? Why are you the only one working to pay all of our bills? Is he spending all of your hard earned money?"

My chest is beating harder, and I feel dizzy. The car drifts to the right, and I jerk the wheel to bring the car back to the middle of the lane.

"I mean, don't you ever wonder what he's been doing? He comes home, what, once every couple of weeks? Where is he going?"

"Shion," I jerk my hand back as her hand touches my arm. "Calm down. What are you talking about?"

"It's him, right? He's the killer. That's the only thing that makes sense. He always says that he has work to do, but then he doesn't come back for days. This week was the most I've seen him in years. Did you know that the day they found Arvir's body, he was gone the whole week?"

"You saw him?"

"He didn't tell you?"

She tilts her head to the side, looking me straight in the eyes. I turn from her to the road several times before she speaks.

"Shion... your dad's dead."

The front tire pulls off the road, and I twist the wheel to pull the car straight.

"What do you mean he's dead?"

Her hands fly up to her face, and she gawks at me. "What are you even asking me? Your dad has been dead ever since we moved here. You haven't seen your dad since you were a year old. He hasn't been coming home or doing anything. And he's definitely not murdering anyone. He's dead, and he's been dead for decades."

"That... that can't be possible. He came to my room. Just a few days ago."

"Shion..."

"He was there! He came to my door, he told me you were worried about me, he knew about the drawings!"

I grip the wheel in my hands, digging my nails into the rubber.

Why is she saying these things?

"Shion... We need to take you somewhere. Get you some help."

"I don't need any help! I need to know what's going on!" My heart is pounding out of my chest.

She thinks I'm lying.

"I saw you a few weeks ago. You were carrying an animal. A dead one. What were you doing with it?"

My lip quivers, and I struggle to open my mouth. "No - nothing... it was just for a school project."

"You can't use that excuse for everything! How stupid do you think I am? Your professor isn't asking you to find dead animals from the forest for a school project. What is the real reason you had it? And why are you drawing pictures of dead people?"

She thinks I did it. She thinks I'm the killer.

"Mom, I know the killer is a necromancer. I've been practicing necromancy to help me find out who is doing all of this. I haven't hurt anyone or anything. All of this, it's so I can help protect the town. To protect my friends. To protect you. I'm not the killer. I swear."

She keeps her gaze fixed on the road in front of us.

"You believe me, right? You have to believe me."

Her voice is low and I can hardly make out what she says. "You're just like your dad."

The rest of the ride is in silence. Nothing more but the cawing of crows above our car as we drive back towards the town.

Chapter 16

"Fasmoh? Where are you going this late?"

My heart drops when I hear Dad's voice coming from the kitchen. I hoped that he wouldn't notice until after I left.

"I'm heading to the academy right now. The scholarship ceremony is tonight, remember? I mentioned it a few months ago."

When I enter the kitchen, he folds up the towel he was using to clean the kitchen table and sets it to the side. He takes a deep breath.

"With everything that has happened, I don't think you should go anywhere. It's not safe for you to be out alone so late at night. Especially with what happened to you and your friends yesterday. And we have lots of work to get done here. What about these dishes? Do you expect me to do these all on my own and then make dinner?"

I look at the pile of dishes stacked in the sink. But I don't recognize most of them.

"Almost all of those are Jhakan's. Why don't you make him do them instead?"

"You know how busy he's been. The Royal Guardians have been working him late every night. All because of this serial killer. He barely has enough time to sleep, let alone take care of dishes."

I know that he's been busy, but it's still not fair.

"Dad, come on! I need to have my own life, I can't just spend all of it taking care of both of you. Why am I the only one expected to pick up all the work Mom used to do?"

I clench my jaw, regretting those words. His head tilts forward.

I want to apologize, but he pivots around before I can. "You're right, go have fun. I'll take care of these tonight. Tomorrow we can discuss house roles."

I watch as he struggles to reach the sink.

Maybe I should stay. But I also want to go to the ceremony. For Ariy.

He looks over his shoulder, a plate in one hand. "How are you getting there? You're not walking, are you?"

"Shion is supposed to pick me up."

"Okay, but make sure he drops you off at the end of the night, too. I don't want you walking alone so late."

I hug him from behind the chair, catching him off guard. His puffy, gray hair tickles my face, and I brush it away with my forehead. His arms fall down to mine.

"Thanks, dad. I love you."

He laughs. "Yeah, yeah. I love you too."

When I get to Shion's house, all the lights are off. I send him a quick text to see where he's at.

It's nearly 10:00. The ceremony is supposed to start in a few minutes, and Shion is nowhere to be found.

He couldn't have forgotten. His memory is too good to forget something like this.

I don't know if I should be mad at him or not. He's the one who offered to drive me.

Maybe his mom is still mad at him about last night. She did sound angry.

Or maybe he thought we weren't planning on going anymore since Ariy was dead.

But then why aren't they at home? Did they go somewhere? Shion and his mom didn't seem to spend a lot of time together.

Could something have happened to them?

I pull out my phone, looking to see if he's read my last few texts yet. No luck.

He's not coming.

Why did I trust him to come get me? He's always so into himself. He never cares much about other people. Not once did he ask how I was doing after Mom's death. Or Ariy's death.

He doesn't care about anyone but himself. And about finding out who the killer is.

A gust of wind passes, causing a chill on the side of my body. I turn to look behind me in the direction it came from. The sidewalk and road are empty. A few house lights are on to illuminate the path. One street light flashes before burning out.

I pick up my pace, walking faster towards the school. The academy isn't too far from here.

Lights wash over me from behind, and I turn to see who it is. It's not Shion's car. I don't recognize it.

"Hello? Who's there?"

The lights turn off, shrouding everything around me in darkness. Someone steps out from the driver's side.

Do I run?

"Fasmoh? Hey, don't worry, it's just me."

Ms. Nula?

"I was driving to the ceremony. Is that where you're going? I can take you there if you would like."

"Oh, uh yeah, sure. Thanks."

I get into the passenger side of the car, and she drives us towards the school. It's much safer watching from the inside.

"How have things been for you? Are you doing all right with everything that's going on?"

I nod. "Mhm. Yeah, things have been a lot better for me this week."

From the side, I can see her smile. "I'm glad. I know you and your mom were close."

Did she? Or is that just a guess?

She continues. "I was wondering if you ever heard. From the Royal Guardians. Did they ever find out who was responsible for her death?"

"What kind of question is that? Do you think this is an appropriate time for you to be talking to me about this?"

"I'm sorry, I'm sorry. I'll drop it." She pauses, bringing her hands back to the wheel. She tapes it with her fingernails. "What are you doing out here on your own?"

"A friend was supposed to take me to the academy tonight."

"Shion?"

"Yeah."

She takes a hand off the wheel and sets it over mine.

"Be careful with him, okay? Something's not right about him. I know he's the one who killed Arvir. I know it."

She looks at me through the side of her eye, waiting for me to respond. But I don't.

"I don't understand it. Arvir's mom keeps talking about how she trusts Shion, and that she knows he could never do something like that. Even after we saw his drawing. I just... I don't understand how she can trust him. She thinks his family is perfect and can't do anything wrong. I don't know what to do."

She shakes her head, turning back to me again.

"You must know what I'm talking about. Haven't you noticed how weird he's been, too?"

Besides the fact that he can summon magical weapons? And has such a vast knowledge of magical traps? But I can't mention any of this. If she finds out he has magic, she might report him.

"I know you're his friend, but promise you won't tell him this? I always knew something was off about them. When he and his mom first moved to town, I knew something was wrong."

"Moved here? You mean he wasn't born here?"

Her nose and forehead scrunch up. "You didn't know? He was born in Eahmore."

I let out an involuntary gasp. Eahmore?

"You have heard the stories about Eahmore, right?"

I shake my head.

"Over twenty years ago, there was a string of murders in Eah-more. Ten, maybe twelve people were slaughtered? There's one that I can never forget. They were looking for a man who had been missing for a few days. They found a handprint on the wall of the basement. Apparently, someone had a hidden portal."

She turns the key in the ignition, shutting off the car. I didn't even notice we stopped.

After a few breaths, she continues. "Inside, they found the man. His body was strung up against a wall. They had tortured him for weeks. The killer kept him alive to torture him. They only killed him because the police were about to find him."

Could those murders be connected to the ones happening here?

"But that couldn't have been him. He would have been a baby."

She purses her lips together. "I'm not saying he was the one responsible for the ones in Eahmore." I look at her, confused. "Magic always runs in the family."

She has a forced smile on her face. Her eyes look tired and sunken. "Just be careful, okay?"

"I will."

When I leave her car, she leans the seat back and closes her eyes.

As I enter the academy, all I can think about is what she said.

Does this mean that Shion's Mom could be the killer? He did say that she's been staying at home more.

When I step inside the cafeteria, I scan the room. A lot of students didn't show up tonight. The only ones I recognize are ones waiting to hear the results of the scholarship awards.

I don't notice Jhakan, either. Only a few of the recently convert-ed Royal Guards are here. The one that was talking to us yesterday isn't here, either.

At least there's free food.

I make my way to the opposite side of the room where the table of food and drinks are. As I approach it, my mouth falls open. My feet freeze to the floor.

Ariy?

Chapter 17

I close my eyes, trying to force myself to fall asleep. But too much is running through my mind.

That was the first nice dinner that we had together. No arguments, no fighting.

At least not until dad came up.

Is he really dead? Does that mean he's not the killer?

I lift Luna's head from my lap, setting her back gently on the bed sheet. She cuddles against the fabric, gripping it in her paws.

When I turn the phone screen on, there are dozens of missed calls and texts. All from Fasmoh. I'm about to scroll through the messages when a call comes through.

"Hello?"

"Why haven't you been answering? I've been texting and calling you nonstop!"

"Sorry, my mom and I went out to eat. I just got back a couple of minutes ago. What's going on?"

"I'm at the awards ceremony. You need to get here. Now."

I forgot I was supposed to drive her. "I'm sorry, we got into an argument and - "

"Just get to the academy. Get here as soon as you can."

"Okay, I'm coming."

I hang up, throwing the phone back into my backpack. Grabbing one of the hoodies from my closet, I pull it over my head before going down the staircase.

Mom's sitting in front of the TV. She doesn't react as I walk to the front door.

"Hey, I'm heading out."

"Okay."

I feel bad. Is this really what our relationship has spiraled into? But I don't have the time to deal with it now. It'll have to wait until later.

Maybe.

I feel the car keys in my pocket. At least I won't have to run.

When I reach the cafeteria of the school, I'm out of breath. I try to find Fasmoh, but she reaches me first.

"Hey, sorry I'm late. Sorry I didn't pick you up, I - "

She points to the crowd. I follow her finger, not sure what she's trying to show me. It's a group of other students, talking to several of the scholarship committee members.

It's Ariy.

"We saw her die. Didn't we?" Fasmoh asks.

I open my mouth to answer when Ariy turns to look at us.

She smiles and waves. Without saying anything to the people around her, she walks over to us. Her hair is curled up, pulled from one side to hang over the other side of her face. She's not wearing her glasses anymore, either.

"Wow, I'm so glad you two could make it. Shion, I was sure you were going to forget about this." Her voice is teasing, and the sound of it makes my chest tighten. She's acting like nothing happened.

Fasmoh grips my arm as she speaks. "Ariy? Are you okay?"

"Of course I'm okay. Why do you ask? You always worry too much. I know I'm going to win that scholarship. I'm the only likely candidate. Don't worry, everything will be okay."

Ariy stares back into my eyes, keeping the smile plastered on her face as the lights dim. She only turns when Ms. Nula stands on stage, clearing her voice into the microphone.

"Hello everyone, and thank you all for coming. I know that with everything going on in the town, people are worried." She stops at the front of the stage before looking up at the crowd. "But that just gives us even more reason to be here today. To honor our exceptional scholars that have made it. Scholars that have given so much of themselves over the years to be awarded this opportunity."

Everyone claps and a few people in the back cheer along. Once it quiets, she continues.

"Remember, this scholarship isn't only for our students. This scholarship is for our town to find the brightest and the best, the ones that can help to protect our town and our people. The ones that can be a part of the Royal Guardians of Coniston. These are who we are here for today."

When the light turns back on, the crowd explodes into applause.

She begins to read off the list of names, starting with the lower award scholarships. The earlier winners seem disappointed.

"And for our final winner of the Honor of the Guard scholarship... Congrats to Ms. Ariy Dhushi!"

Fasmoh and I are the only ones not clapping.

Ariy walks up the stairs on the side of the stage, reaching out to shake Ms. Nula's hand. They pause for a picture. The flash is bright, and Ariy's face freezes in a smile for a moment. Ms. Nula tries to pull away, and Ariy clenches it before letting go.

"What's wrong with her?"

Before I can respond, Ariy speaks.

"I just want to say thank you so much for giving me this opportunity. You have no idea what this award means to me or to my family."

She wipes away at the corners of her eyes. But I know it's fake.

"The only jobs my parents could find took them away from me. They have to work in another town just to support me. Because they believe in me. They believe I could do this and win. That I could make something of myself."

A group of guards roars, shaking the table with their fists. She looks at them with a cryptic smile on her face. Though that makes the guards yell louder, my heart beats harder.

"It was all thanks to the Royal Guardians that I am here today. I am here today because of you. It is your incompetence that has allowed me to rise above the rest."

Whispers start to sound throughout the audience, and I hear someone ask a friend what she said. Her voice raises, silencing the room.

"How long does it take for the guards to respond to a call about a break-in? Does three hours sound right? Because that's how long it took before someone finally came to help me." She lets out a laugh. "After that night, I promised myself. I promised myself that I would do whatever it takes to become strong. To be able to protect myself. In a way that none of you were able to."

Ms Nula steps forward, reaching for the microphone. "Ariy, stop. Please, give me the microphone. We can talk about this later."

But Ariy pulls away from her.

"And you, Ms. Nula. I have you to thank most of all. Because even though you've always known how corrupt the Royal Guardians are, you continue to push the students into it. You continue to force us to learn how to be perfect, obedient workers. How to be one of them."

Ms. Nula's head snaps backwards. Her hands claw at her neck.

The people in the front closest to the stage start to stand at their tables. Everyone backs away, some heading towards the exits.

"Shion? What's happening? What is she doing?"

I can't turn away.

Ariy's shadow is reaching out from hers to Ms. Nula's, covering it. It rises from the ground, spreading to the walls and ceiling. Long, dark limbs emerge from both sides of the shadow, creating jagged arms.

It slashes downward, right through the middle of Ms. Nula's body. She wavers back and forward, and a line of blood appears.

Her body splits, each half falling to opposite sides.

By now, the room is in chaos. People are screaming and shoving each other, trying to get to the exits. Someone slams their shoulder against a door, but it doesn't budge.

"Shion!"

My body freezes. Ariy steps up to another man, touching his shoulder with a light hand. His body contorts, face looking similar to how Ms. Nula's was. Only the whites of his eyes are visible.

But instead of getting ripped in two, his shadow rises up to meet Ariy's. The two twist around each other before returning to their owners.

His head falls forward. The bright green of his eyes darts back and forward before dilating. The color in his eyes starts to swirl, transforming into a deep red.

His back snaps, pulling his body to the side. The bones crack over the sounds of the screams.

The bones from his spine start to rip through his back. They fan outward and reach towards the ground, lifting the rest of his lifeless body into the air.

His mouth opens, letting out a loud, inhuman wail. Lifting one of his new bone limbs, he stabs it through the face of a nearby woman. Her body folds backwards to the floor. Her legs twitch a few times.

Ariy notices us, face twisting up into a crooked grin.

"Fasmoh, Shion. Join me. Together, we'll be powerful."

Fasmoh's body shakes next to mine..

I'm the one who replies. "Ariy, look at what you're doing to everyone. This isn't power, this is evil. You're tormenting them."

Her smile turns into a smirk. "That's rich, coming from you. You've had magic for a while, and you were too selfish to share it with anyone. Not even with us, your best friends. You were hoarding the power for yourself, and you didn't care when we needed it."

"Move!" Fasmoh pulls me away from Ariy towards one of the back windows. Several others are trying to climb them, but more of those creatures stop them. Grabbing their legs and dragging them further down before killing them.

Some change, just like the man from before. Others die.

I shove Fasmoh up on my shoulders, and she pulls herself onto the ledge. She twists the handle, trying to push the window open.

"It won't open!"

While the other monsters seem to be ignoring us, Ariy has her eyes set. She steps over the bodies and blood, closing the gap between us.

"Ariy, who did this to you? What happened in the Reflecting Pools?"

But she ignores my questions.

"If you won't join me, then I'll just have to take your powers for myself."

Her shadow extends outward and lifts from the ground. The darkness closes in around my body.

"No!"

Fasmoh's voice travels with her as she jumps from the window, landing between the two of us.

She throws her right arm forward, and a bright light emits from where her right hand used to be. It connects with Ariy's stomach.

Ariy and her shadow are thrown backwards, slamming against one of the folding tables. They crash to the floor.

Fasmoh stands there, looking down with confusion at her arm. She doesn't notice another one of the creatures coming towards her.

It's a bright green liquid, and while it still resembles the shape of the woman it turned from, it flops around boneless on the ground. One limb reaches forward, and the back side lifts up, rolling over the limb. It reaches forward again, leaving a trail of neon green behind it.

I drag Fasmoh over to the opposite end of the room, stepping over the bodies piled near the door.

Something catches my eye. It's faint, but when I squint I can see it. A wispy layer of red covers the door and wall.

I conjure a dagger in my hand, slamming the tip directly into the layer of mist. As the blade goes through, it dissipates from the door. I push it open and hurry Fasmoh through first before turning back.

The green blob squelches against the floor, following behind us. It's much larger now. It drags its body over a guard who had fallen to the floor.

The arm suspends in the center of its green body and starts to bubble. The skin and flesh fizz away, leaving only exposed bone. He cries out, reaching his free hand out.

The blob ignores him.

He yells louder as the creature slams his body against a hanging light as it rolls towards me. His other arm rips from his body as the creature throws him against the ground.

I close the door, joining Fasmoh in the hallway.

"We need to get out of here. If we want to stop this, all of this, we have to find out who was the one who turned Ariy into that thing."

Luckily, the barrier only blocked the inside of the cafeteria. The back door looks free.

I reach forward to grab the door handle. Before I can, a piercing pain shoots through my stomach and back before spreading through the rest of my body.

Fasmoh screams.

Chapter 18

I f I can just reach it.

But I can't move. I'm paralyzed. It's as if the black mass below me is siphoning the strength from my body.

"Shion!" Fasmoh holds a shaking hand up to my cheek. "Are you okay?"

But I can't respond.

Fasmoh moves around me, careful not to come into contact with any of the dark spike.. Through the reflection on the window, Ariy walks toward us.

Please... please look up.

I try to catch Fasmoh's attention with my eyes, but they won't move. I can barely blink.

Fasmoh...

She doesn't notice until Ariy is standing right next to her.

Her back slams against the door. She shrinks away from Ariy's outstretched hand.

"Isn't this what you wanted? To have magic? We've spent so long practicing together, and we finally have it! It's so much more than we thought it could ever be. Please, share it with me."

Fasmoh presses her back against the wall and holds her eyes shut. Her entire body trembles.

Ariy pleads. "Don't you remember? Who was the only one there for you when your mom died? Not your dad, not your brother, not Shion. Me. I was the only one who was there for you. I'm the only one who knows how to make you happy."

She leans over Fasmoh, mouth right next to her ear. "I can make it all better. I can even bring your mom back to you. Don't you want to see her again? You would never have to be apart. Ever."

Fasmoh rises to her feet, and Ariy takes a step back.

"Everyone in there - the Dean, the guards. You killed them all, Ariy. They have families, too. Can't you see the kind of monster you're turning into? I would never want to become like that, to become like you."

"But that's the great thing! You won't have to change. Not like the others. I can keep you the same. And none of them will try to hurt you. You would be one of us. We wouldn't let anyone hurt you."

"I understand that you're hurt. I know how you feel about them. How much you hate them." Fasmoh closes her eyes, trying to find the right words. "But that doesn't mean you can do this. This isn't just revenge, not any more. Those people had families, kids. Most of them weren't even involved in what happened!"

"You of all people are defending this place? These people are evil. They deserve this. You were the one who always talked about how useless and corrupt the Royal Guardians are." Ariy forces out a short laugh. "At least until they took your brother in."

Fasmoh's eyes fall to the floor and she pauses for a few moments. Her breathing deepens, and she falls back against the glass. "This isn't about Jhakan. This is about you. You hurt so many people, so many of our friends and classmates. Are you going to kill everyone who stands against you? This isn't right."

"Everyone's a part of this, Fasmoh. Everyone. The students, the school, the guard. All of them. And I'm the only one strong enough to stand against them."

She steps forward, holding a hand out to Fasmoh once more. For the first time, I notice the shakiness in her voice. "It was supposed to be you and me together forever. I can't do this without you. I need you, Fasmoh. Together, we can fix everything."

My body slides down the spike. My legs and arms are numb. With each blink, it becomes harder to open my eyes.

Please Fasmoh, please don't trust her. If you can hear me, please don't do this. She's lying.

Fasmoh reaches forward and grabs Ariy's hand..

Right as she does, Ariy screams. The scream sounds normal at first, but it raises higher until it's an inhuman shriek. Crystals of ice grow up her arm from her hand, soon spreading to her shoulders.

Small red thorns emerge from her free hand, and she shoves them into her arm. They pierce the ice, revealing blood as she pulls away. She does this a few more times, and pieces of ice shatter on the floor.

She stabs one last time at the ice, breaking large pieces from it. Her arm is free.

"You will pay for that! You were supposed to be my best friend!"

Thin bony wings rip out from each side of her spine. The jagged tips dig themselves into the walls and ceiling surrounding Fasmoh.

Fasmoh shrinks into the corner of the wall, and I can see her fear. She cowers away from the creature that used to be our friend.

No matter how hard I try, I can't move. Even as Ariy's head snaps backwards, splitting open at the mouth. I still can't move.

I watch helplessly as her body splits open wider at the neck, nearly separating the top of her head from the bottom. She tilts her head forward, slamming it in Fasmoh's direction.

At the last moment, Fasmoh's face stiffens, and she ducks underneath Ariy's gaping mouth. Ariy's head hits the wall, dazing her.

In Fasmoh's missing hand, a red ball of flame expands, turning into a mini fist of fire. She throws it upward into Ariy's stomach, burning a hole all the way through to her back. Ariy falls backwards against the floor.

"Oh my god, look, look Shion!" Her mouth is in a wide grin and she holds her hand out to me. Her face falls in realization, and she looks down.

"I… I don't know what to do." She looks at her fiery fist, concentrating on it for a few seconds. The flame dissipates and is replaced by a growing bright light. As she brings it closer to the spike, the darkness squirms away from her fist.

She touches it, and my body falls to the floor.

The energy rushes back into my body. I can move again.

"Can you walk?"

I shake the numbness from my body before flashing her a thumbs up.

"We need to go! They're breaking through."

She points towards one of the door frames crushing under a massive weight. Something slams down on it, sending the metal door flying into the lockers on the opposite wall.

A long, blue arm reaches on both sides of the doorway. As it pulls itself, it reveals its bright blue body. A skeletal arm is stuck inside of the jelly-like body.

"Shion! Come on!"

"Give me a minute."

I brush her hand off of mine, pulling a small dagger out. Kneeling over her body, I hold the dagger above my head and close my eyes.

Chapter 19

"What are we doing here?" Fasmoh's voice is in a whisper. She looks around the room before her gaze settles on the staircase. "It's her, isn't it?"

I wonder what makes her suspect Mom, too.

"Just give me a few minutes with her. Alone. I'll figure out what's going on."

I turn up to the staircase, looking at her door. "Mom? Are you home?"

The house is silent. The only light in the house is the one we turned on when we entered.

"Wait here. I'll go up on my own."

Fasmoh nods, and I hurry up the stairs to her bedroom. I throw the door open.

"Mom?"

She's sitting on the edge of her bed, looking at the floor. When I burst in, she doesn't turn.

"Mom? Are you okay?" I take a few steps forward, seeing her arms.

They're covered in blood. Her shirt, her pants, and her sleeves have blood smeared on the front.

"What happened? Did someone try to hurt you?"

"I... I had to protect you."

I follow her gaze, finally seeing what she's been staring at the whole time.

It's Guardian Vahreld. He's laying on his back beside the bed, blood gushing from his mouth and chest. There are several stab wounds on his body. The bloody knife sits on the nearby night-stand.

My breath catches in my throat, and I lean back against the door. I push it shut behind me, not wanting to alert Fasmoh.

"You did this, didn't you? You're the killer."

"He came for you. He wanted to blame you for those deaths. I couldn't let that happen." She looks up at me, and her eyes are filled with tears. "Even if you did kill all of those people... I can't let them take you away. I can't let them think you're a monster."

"Mom... Officer Vahreld wasn't trying to blame me for the mur-ders. He knew I didn't do it. He wasn't trying to investigate me, he was trying to help me clear my name. To protect me."

Her eyes widen. Her head shakes back and forward before she turns back to him.

"No... no, it can't be." She drops to her knees, placing her fore-head on his. Wrapping her arms around his body, she pulls him close to her chest.

"I'm so sorry Vilon, I'm so sorry. You were the only one there for me."

She sobs quietly into his chest.

I need to know what happened. She has answers, something that will help me figure everything out. But I can't press her, not when she's like this.

I shuffle side to side on my feet, unsure of what to do. Luckily, her sobs die down and she lifts her head.

"You know your father is dead. But I didn't tell you how he died."

She turns, and I keep quiet to let her continue.

"I killed him."

"You killed him? Why?"

"When we were in Eahmore, you were only a child. One night, there was an accident. You... Well, you died. I don't know exactly what happened, but when I came back from work one day, you were just dead. Your dad said he didn't know what happened."

I died? Does that mean I was resurrected?

"Your father, he thought what he was doing was right. He quit his job and spent his time learning necromancy. But, he couldn't just learn it by reading or watching videos. He had to practice."

She closes her eyes, taking a deep breath.

"I didn't want to believe it. When the first murder happened, everyone thought it was an accident. I thought it was an accident. But then a few nights after the murder, I walked in on him in his basement. Usually he locked the door, but one night I guess he forgot. I saw him, Shion. He was doing stuff to the body. Cutting it up, desecrating it. It was a nightmare. I didn't know what to do."

"That's why you killed him? Because he was a murderer?"

A tear streams down the side of her cheek, and she wipes it away. "Not at first. I thought that maybe he'd stop, or that he would change his mind. But he didn't. Not until you came back. But by then, he wasn't satisfied. He wanted more."

"What does this have to do with the murders here in Coniston?"

"I... I don't know. Deep down, I thought it was you. I thought somehow his magic changed you, or corrupted you." Her hands start to tremble and she grips her legs in her arms. "I was just trying to protect you."

I kneel beside her, holding her hands in mine. "Mom, I promise you. I am not the one hurting people. I've been trying to find out who the killer was."

"Then why are you practicing necromancy?"

I close my eyes. If I want to find out exactly what's happening, I need to tell her.

"There's a spell that the killer has been using. At first it was a resurrection spell, but the killer changed it, combined it with something somehow. I need that spell. I need to know what it does, how it works. If we can figure out how he's using it to corrupt the living, then we might be able to stop him. Otherwise, the corruption might spread throughout the entire world."

"A resurrection spell?"

She stands, stepping next to the bed. "Help me with this."

We drag the bed to the opposite side of the room. Underneath, bloody handprints stain a small area of the wood.

She pulls the knife from her nightstand and uses it to cut her finger. Her arm hangs as she quickly sketches a pattern on the floor. A small wooden chest appears in the center of the blood.

She struggles with the small padlock, and it clicks open. From inside, she pulls out a rolled out scroll.

"I think this might be the spell you are looking for."

The scroll has instructions. I read each of the ingredients and procedures several times. On the back is the pattern. I look at it for a few seconds, and close my eyes, keeping the picture in my vision. I open and close them a few more times before turning back to her.

"Why do you have this?"

Her head drops. "I found this. Among your dad's things after he... died. I didn't know what it did or what it meant, but I just couldn't throw it away."

I hand the scroll back to her and she grabs it, letting it fall to the floor.

"So what now? Are you going to turn me into the Royal Guard?"

I shake my head. "I have to go."

"Will I see you again?"

Her words catch me off guard, and I look over my shoulder. She's still on the floor, looking up at me with sullen eyes.

My heart aches for her. I've never seen her look so broken.

"Goodbye, Mom."

When I leave her bedroom, she doesn't follow me. She doesn't even move.

I look between the staircase and dad's room. I know I need to hurry and get back to Wanderlust.

But I also need to know.

The door slowly creaks open. Behind it, the room is completely empty. No table, no chair, no bed, nothing. As if no one's ever lived there.

By the time I get back to the first floor, Fasmoh is sitting on the bench next to the front door, waiting. She turns as she hears my steps.

"Was it her?"

"No."

She sucks air through her teeth, hitting her head against the wall behind her. "So what are we supposed to do now? How can we end this?"

"There's nothing more we can do. I have what I need to end this."

She jumps up from her seat. "What do we need to do?"

I look to the floor and scratch the back of my neck. "We don't do anything. We've done everything we needed to do. There's nothing more you can do to help. I - I really can't explain right now. I need to go."

She holds the door shut, blocking my pathway.

"What do you mean, you can't explain it to me? You said you'd tell me everything. Now you're just going to leave? You told me you were going to do better. That you would be a better friend. You can't just leave me like this, not when we're so close to ending this."

She holds up her missing hand. Her voice quivers.

"Why don't I matter to you?"

I hate how much I've hurt her. How much I've hurt everyone.

"Fasmoh, you do matter to me. You have no idea how much you matter to me. But I need to leave. So that I can end this. To protect everyone. I'm the only one who can stop this."

She grabs my wrist, gripping it. Her face comes close, close enough that her breath tickles my face. "Then let me help you. I'll come with you. We can end this together. You just need to tell me what's happening. Why won't you let me understand?"

"Fasmoh, please - "

"I won't let you leave without telling me."

We stand in a deadlock, staring each other down. But there's no other way out of this. I have to tell her.

"If you think I don't care about what's going on, well, then I guess you're right. I don't care. None of these deaths means anything."

Her gaze narrows.

"I don't care, because I can't care. Because none of this matters." My chest tightens, and my eye jerks to the door. I'm certain I can force my way through the door.

But I have to tell her. I can't leave it at this.

"Have you ever seen Kalansa? At Wanderlust?"

She thinks over the name before responding. "I never met her, but I heard stories about her from the other students. Some say that she can bring people back in time or something like that."

She inhales a quick gasp.

"I visited her. To come back here. To come back here to find the killer and find out how he's been doing this. It turns out my mom is the one who had the spell. Now that I have it, we can stop him. I can go back to help them stop him."

Her mouth falls open. "You... you mean..."

I nod. Her face falls, and I can see her struggling to understand the situation. Her hands go up to her face, and she grips her head tightly.

"Fasmoh…" I reach a hand out to her, but she pulls away. Her eyes are wild and her body tense.

"So all of this already happened?"

She notices my silence. "So none of this matters."

There's nothing more I can say to comfort her.

"Goodbye, Shion."

Chapter 20

I want to chase after her, to stop her. To tell her that everything will be fine.

But I can't. I can't lie to her again.

She takes off in the opposite direction from her house. Towards the school.

It doesn't matter. Now that I understand how the spell works, there's no reason for me to stay here. It's time for me to return.

I decide to take the long way. I don't know if it's the thought of seeing Kalansa again, or if it's because this will probably be my last time in the forest again.

In the clearing where Arvir's body was, I lift my head to the tree tops. Almost all of Arvir's body parts are gone from the trees, except for the ones near the very tops.

The wind blows, ruffling the surrounding leaves. A chill crawls up my spine.

It's dark. The sun is already gone.

Before I can take another step forward, a dark mist floats in front of me. It circles, sending dirt and debris into the air. I cover my eyes to protect them from the mini whirlwind.

When I can finally see, there's an outline in front of me. It's a shadowy figure with the shape of a person. It lifts its head, but it has no eyes and no face.

"Shion." Its voice is wispy and soft.

"Dad?"

The faceless head widens, as if grinning.

"So you know. And you still choose to stand against me?"

"I'm trying to help protect the people from you. You and those creatures, you're destroying this town. You've hurt people. You've hurt me. I will do anything I can to stop you from corrupting everyone."

The figure tilts its head back to laugh.

"The academy, the school, the town. They're the ones who have corrupted you. Look at how easily they were able to turn you against the ones who care about you, who want to help you. They trained you well."

"No one trained me. I know everything you've done, and everything you are going to do. Look at the people you killed. You are evil, and I want nothing more to do with you."

He flinches at my words, offended.

"If I'm evil, then all hope for you is lost."

He raises an arm. Claws line the bottom until it reaches a long, sharp point. The arm swipes to the side, digging itself into the trunk of a nearby tree.

The two halves fall to the ground, and a brown vine rips up from the center. I fall back, ducking behind a tree trunk as rocks and dirt hit the ground around me.

From around the corner of the tree, I can see it.

A decayed tree hovers in the air, held up by multiple thorny legs. The right side of its body is blackened and charred. Slash marks line one side of its face where something ripped it. On the other side is a bright red eye.

In its burned tree branch, it holds a bright swirling ball of gray and green light. It lifts it before throwing it in my direction.

As it approaches, the tree around me starts to decay. Pieces of the trunk break off, falling to my sides. Once it's gone, my body falls back. The skin on my arm fades. Pieces flake away as it dries.

I hear small feet running from my side, and something jumps towards the ball. When they collide, the thing suspends in the air. It absorbs the green light, ripping away at it. Once the light is gone, the thing falls to the dirt.

Luna.

Patches of bloody flesh and skin cover his body. It looks like parts of him had been poorly reattached.

Through a gap in his chest, I can see his heart beat with difficulty.

"Why did you follow me? I told you to stay back at the house!"

His eyes drop forward. His heart beats twice, squirting out two spurts of blood.

He's gone.

I shouldn't feel anything. None of this matters. He doesn't matter.

But my heart hurts.

I've lost everyone.

By the time I raise my head, my dad is standing over me. The creature hovers above him, waiting for his command.

His face widens in a grin. "You've learned resurrection already? You possess so much more power than I had thought. Imagine what we could accomplish. Together."

I lunge forward, swiping the dagger in front of me. But he vanishes.

Something hard slams into my ribs, sending my body flying across the floor. The dagger falls from my hand as my back hits a tree.

The impact sends a shock through my body. I struggle to stand, but my legs wobble under my weight.

His body reappears in front of me, and he walks towards me.

The dagger. It's so close, but my entire body is sore. I can't even lift my arm without it burning.

He's close. His breath burns on my face.

"I will give you one last chance. Join me, and together we can take control of the town. We can be in control for once. We can be a family again."

In the silence, he smirks. "It's okay. You don't have to agree to it. But either way, you'll be with us."

The creature raises another ball of green behind us. The ground cracks. Grass turns from brown to gray before disappearing.

With my last bit of strength, I dig my nails into my palms, piercing the skin. I throw myself forward. Black shadowy tendrils rip out of his chest. Several of them dig into my chest and abs, pushing me backwards.

They dig deeper as I shove my weight forward, forcing my body closer to his.

He pushes back against me, sending out several more tendrils. One pierces through my shoulder, and my hand falls.

I have to do this.

Rising my head to face him, I use my last bit of strength to take one small step forward.

As I fall to the ground, my hand passes through his leg.

He pulls away, and I gasp as the tendrils rip from my body.

The red blood from my palm flicks out at him. Trails of blood lift, wrapping themselves around him.

He screams, pulling away.

Fog circles around him. The blood and fog mix, sealing him in a cocoon of black and red.

The creature behind him roars. New branches break from the decaying body, holding green leaves.

The cocoon wraps around his body, closing in on him.

Once it's about the size of my fist, it pops, leaving a puddle of blood.

My body fades. I close my eyes.

CHAPTER 21

My eyelids flutter and I open my eyes. When I do, smoke blocks my vision. I cough, trying to clear it from my lungs. It has a woody, earthy taste.

Kalansa sits across from me. She looks frail and wrinkles cover her hands. Creases line her face.

"You have returned."

"Yeah. Finally."

She knits her eyebrows together. "How was your return? It was not a calm one."

I notice the broken glass on the side of the table. "Sorry about that. Someone killed me."

"Ah yes. Another way to return. Not as easy, but it works. So you did not go see Kalansa then?"

"I wasn't trying to, but it was an accident. I swear. To find the killer, we were at Wanderlust, and I accidentally ran into her. I'm sorry."

I thought she would be angry that I didn't follow her rules, but she's not. Instead, a small smile crosses her face. "You do not need to apologize, it matters not. I only ask because I was curious. When you saw her, how did she react? What did she do?"

"She was angry. She went crazy and told me I had to go back. That I wasn't welcome there anymore."

She nods and crosses her arms. "Once she saw you, she realized what happened. Who she was. She needed to get rid of you." She stands, opening the front door for me. "I believe the guards are still waiting for you."

"Thank you, Kalansa."

After taking a few steps, I turn back. It's so much different now.

Instead of a flimsy tent in the front, there's another room attached to the front of her shop. The building is taller now, and it looks like the walls had been torn down to make the building wider.

Hers is the only building left. The others around it have been demolished. Broken pieces of wood and glass pile on the sidewalk and streets.

"Mr. Kuen, are you ready to leave?" The driver's voice calls from the street. He holds the door open for me as I duck in.

Guardian Vahreld sits on the seat across from me.

"Hello, Shion. Were you able to find out the information we requested?"

I nod.

"Good."

He pulls out a notebook, scribbling away as I explain everything to him. Who the killer was, how the resurrection spell worked.

When I get to the pattern, he passes the notebook to me. I scribble the drawing of the symbol before passing it back.

"We're here."

Outside my window, my apartment complex faces us. The white paint on the walls is faded, and portions of it are ripped.

I'm back.

As I climb the left staircase, the car waits for me at the bottom.

I rest my hand against the door, trying to find the courage.

I knock on the door.

Within a second, the door opens.

It's her. Her piercing dark eyes stare into mine. Besides her short haircut, she looks exactly the same.

"Mom, hey, how are - "

"Look who finally decided to come back. What do you want?"

"I - I'm just here to pick up my things."

She smacks her hand against her forehead in surprise. "Oh, that's right, they're letting you out of this shithole, huh? Well go on, be quick. Your stuff is waiting for you. Someone's coming to replace you soon."

My lack of response seems to catch her off guard. I can tell she wants to say something more, but she stops herself and steps to the side.

I step over the shoes at the entrance. The living room is more crowded than before.

It's only been a day since I've been gone, but it feels much longer.

Most of the others are laying in their bunk beds. But none of them pay attention to me.

She already turned them against me.

Khadeem is the only one who turns to me. But before I can say anything, his mom grabs him and pulls him into the bed. She grabs the curtain surrounding the bottom bunk, closing it shut.

At the end of the living room, my old bed is waiting for me. Packing takes less than a minute. The whole time I can feel them watching me from behind.

When I return to the entrance, she's still waiting by the open door.

"I hope you don't forget anything. Wouldn't want to have to come back here, right?"

Before, I would have made a snarky response. But I don't. Not anymore.

The small spark of hope in me that thought she might have kept the memories we shared is gone. She doesn't remember any of it. She never will. Only I will.

"Goodbye, Mom."

I snap my mouth shut. The confusion on her face reminds me I haven't called her that in years.

She slams the door in my face, and the lock clicks. I turn, walking back to the car.

We sit in silence as the car drives us up the hill towards the back of town.

The new house looks the same as the pictures Vahreld showed me when he offered me this quest. I didn't care what it looked like, though. All I needed was to get out of that apartment. Away from her.

From the outside, it's much bigger than the apartment.

Vahreld hands me a key ring. When the door opens, I move to it. He grabs me by the wrist and I turn to him.

"Did you think over my offer?"

"Give me more time, please. After all of this, I just really need a break.

His hand falls, and he smiles. "Of course. I'm sorry. You've done such an amazing thing for the Royal Guardians. And for your town."

I close the door and walk towards the house. The window rolls down and I pause.

"Just don't forget, your stay here is not forever. You will want to decide before then."

I watch as the car pulls away, not breaking my stare until I hear a voice call.

Fasmoh is standing on the balcony, arms crossed, leaning over the railing.

"Shion! You made it! Does that mean you found it? Relli says that's the only reason we'd see you."

She still has her right hand.

"Yeah, I did. I found a lot."

About the Author

Ang Roffe is a writer of horror and fantasy. This book was written to share some of the weird and creepy stories in his head. But as he continued to write, he realized the book was a reflection of his own life.

As a child, Ang had difficulties understanding emotions. He had difficulty fitting in with peers and understanding the feelings of others. Because of this, he has had difficulty holding meaningful relationships. Writing *Obsession* him learn these necessary social emotional skills that he didn't get to learn.

Coming Soon

Ang Roffe's Online Presence
https://sleekbio.com/angroffe

Sign up for the mailing list in the link above to get updates on future books in the series:

Memories of Sorrow Book 2

Memories of Sorrow Book 3